HEADING SOUTH

translated by **Wayne Grady**

HEADING

SOUTH

Dany Laferrière

DOUGLAS & McINTYRE
Vancouver/Toronto/Berkeley

Douglas & McIntyre
An imprint of D&M Publishers Inc.
2323 Quebec Street, Suite 201
Vancouver BC Canada V5T 4S7
www.douglas-mcintyre.com

Library and Archives Canada Cataloguing in Publication
Laferrière, Dany
[Vers le sud. English]
Heading south / Dany Laferriere ; translated by Wayne Grady.
Originally published in 2006 under title: Vers le sud.

ISBN 978-1-55365-483-4

1. Grady, Wayne 11. Title: Vers le sud. English.
PS8573.A348V4713 2009   C843'.54   C2009-903757-2

Copy editing by Pam Robertson
Cover and text design by Peter Cocking
Cover photograph by Steve Vaccariello/Getty Images
Printed and bound in Canada by Friesens
Printed on acid-free paper that is forest friendly (100% post-consumer recycled paper) and has been processed chlorine free
Distributed in the U.S. by Publishers Group West

We gratefully acknowledge the financial support of the Canada Council for the Arts, the British Columbia Arts Council, the Province of British Columbia through the Book Publishing Tax Credit and the Government of Canada through the Book Publishing Industry Development Program (BPIDP) for our publishing activities.

Afternoon of a Faun

I AM SEVENTEEN years old (although because of my size and my easygoing nature I look much older) and I live in Port-au-Prince, on Capois Street, near Place du Champ-de-Mars. I live with my mother and my young sister. My father died a few years ago. My mother is still very beautiful. Large, moist eyes, bright flushed cheeks and a sad smile. The kind of tragic beauty that is very attractive to men. But as they say, she is a one-man woman. My father was not handsome (we have a large photograph of him in the living room), but he was tall and elegant. He always wore white and changed his shirt at least three times a day. They say women were crazy about him, which drove my mother to despair. According to her, what made my father different from other men was his great sensitivity and his keen sense of responsibility. "I can always count on your father," my mother would say every time I forgot to do something. As far as she is concerned, my father is still alive. She talks about him every day. She quotes him every chance she gets. If I come home a bit late on a Friday night, my mother never fails to point out that I behave badly only because my father isn't there. She never says because he's dead. My mother talks so frequently about my father that often I find myself thinking as she does. Some days, at around two o'clock in the afternoon, a feeling comes over me that he's about to walk into the house and, as was his invariable custom, toss his hat onto the table.

"Madeleine, I'm hungry."

"What have you been up to, then?" my mother would reply, smiling.

And he would sit down at the table and wolf down his dinner. No one ate faster than my father. After eating, he would take a short siesta. It was forbidden for us to make the slightest sound while he was resting. At five o'clock sharp he would go out the door and the house would return to normal.

My mother has never accepted his death, but I wasn't always like her in that regard. At times I was even glad that he was no longer around to prevent me from living my life. In a way, my situation wasn't so different from that of my friends. Most of them never knew their fathers (killed, imprisoned or just gone off). At least mine hadn't died in prison. We were all brought up by our mothers. My mother lost her job shortly after my father's death. She had been a junior clerk in the National Archives, behind Saint-Martial College. Now she works as a seamstress, at home. My sister is two years younger than I am. She goes to a snooty private school whose principal is one of my mother's clients. It's only because of this connection that my sister is allowed into her chic school. My mother insisted on it, because she wanted my sister to make "good contacts for later," as she puts it. In a country like Haiti, where the rich barricade themselves in their fancy houses up on the mountainside, the only place we poor folk ever get to mingle with them and make connections is in the classroom. That's what my mother says. In any case, unlike me, my sister does well in school. And despite the two years' difference in our ages, she's the one who always does my homework. Everywhere she goes—before the chic college she went to the Lycée de Jeunes Filles—she quickly becomes the pet of all the teachers. And since she is very giving, which is to say she does all her friends' homework for them, no one gets jealous. As for me, I'm not ashamed to say that school was never my thing. Honestly, I don't see the point in going to school. Only poor people like us knock their heads against the wall trying to solve airy-fairy problems that have nothing to do with real life. And after all these years of school I don't see that it has done them any good at all. People are rich because their parents are rich, it's as simple as that. And their parents are rich because their grandparents were rich. And so on. And when you get down to the source of all that richness, you'll always find someone who made their fortune by robbing from the public purse. That's Haiti for you, and it's not my job to change the way this country is run. My sister got her intelligence from my father. Me, mostly what I got is his size. "You're going to be as tall as your father," my mother often tells me. And I get my delicate features from my mother. I have always been popular with girls. Ever since I was twelve I've known that I could do what I wanted with women. That's just the way it is. Nothing anyone can do about it. My sister's friends are always giving me the once-over—some of them are bolder about it than others—but girls don't interest me very much. I like my women more mature. I like watching them lose their cool. Especially those who take themselves seriously. For some time now I've had my eye on a really choice bird: the principal of the school my sister goes to. I always make sure I'm home when she comes to see my mother for fittings. I don't do a thing. I know she's a respectable person, but I want to see her private side, what's hidden behind her mask, the dark side of her moon. So I sit very still in the room. I know she's spotted me. I've often caught her looking at me out of the corner of her eye. I play the innocent. I pretend I have no idea what's going on. I put on my angelic face, my mother's features. Except that my mother, as my father used to say, is a saint. I'm not. I'm rotten inside. I'm like a spider crouching at the edge of its web, waiting for prey.

My mother has just rushed out of the house to visit a sick friend who called her for help. She asked me to explain her absence to Madame Saint-Pierre, who is supposed to come at two o'clock this afternoon. My sister has gone to a friend's house in Pétionville to study for her second-term exams. She won't be back before four. And then she has to join my mother at the hospital, the Canapé Vert. So I have at least two hours at my disposal. I take a Carter Brown from the little bookshelf. I turn the pages mechanically, passing the time. The trap is set. Waiting is the hardest part. I get up, take a few deep breaths, then go out into the yard. A dead rat near the cistern. I give it a swift kick that propels it into the yard of the next-door neighbour, a kid of about twelve with the brains of a two-year-old.

Afternoon of a Faun

I smile at him and wave. He stares at me like I'm some kind of celestial apparition. Maybe he's not seeing me at all. A car stops in front of the house. Two o'clock on the dot.

She's a punctual lady. I open the door.

"My mother has gone to see a sick friend."

"Oh!" she says, her voice deep and musical. "I hope it's nothing serious."

"I don't know, madame, she didn't tell me what it was."

"Did she tell you when she would be back?"

"No, but I don't think she'll be late."

"Well, then, I'll wait for a bit."

And so she has decided to stay.

"Not that chair, madame, it's not very solid. Sit here, you'll be more comfortable."

She sits on the edge of her seat. Her way of letting me know that she has twigged to my little game and she isn't going to give me a lot of her time. I, in turn, do not fall for that: I already know that whoever controls time wins. I sit down calmly, across from her. I have all the time in the world. I look her straight in the eye, which I have not done to this point. And then I attack.

"Your dress suits you very well, madame."

"Your mother is an excellent seamstress, it's true."

She wants me to go on.

"It's the yellow that suits you, madame."

Which is the limit of insolence. But my innocent face (wide-open eyes, bright smile) saves me. She blushes. I lower my gaze. A bit troubled.

"Your mother is very brave," she says suddenly, to regain her composure.

I must renew my attack immediately.

"It is my opinion that in their own way, all women are brave," I say, looking again into her eyes.

And again she blushes. She now understands that something is going on. I smile at her. Clearly she hasn't expected such a volley from the son of her seamstress, a boy with such sincerity in his eyes and such openness in his smile (or so I've been led to believe, anyway). But I've been playing this game since I was twelve. If I'd been playing tennis this long I'd be going to championships around the world by now. I love tennis, but it's too expensive. I can spend hours watching the endless matches through the green fence at the Bellevue Circle. Madame Saint-Pierre is watching me without smiling. She appears to have grasped something. What has she understood? That despite her intimidating behaviour and her social status (principal of a prestigious school), I have absolutely no fear of her. Not only am I not afraid of her, but I am playing with her as a cat plays with a mouse. She is vexed. She leans forward on her chair, putting on the severe expression with which she intimidates the parents of her students. But it is too late. In this game, there are no second chances. A long moment of silence. We stare at one another. She, furious. Me, calm.

"I don't think I can wait much longer... You'll tell your mother that I was here..."

"Of course," I say, without standing up.

Afternoon of a Faun

She stands for a moment at the centre of the room, her arms hanging by her sides.

Like a ship becalmed.

"Tell her I was here," she says again, moving towards the door.

The back of her neck.

I get up quickly. Like a tiger in an urban jungle. She hesitates for a quarter of a second with her hand ready to turn the handle of the door. I go up to her and lightly brush the back of her neck. She stops dead. I don't move. I see the muscles in her jaw contract. Her hand turns the doorknob. Her body stiffens. With the tips of my fingers I caress the back of her neck once more, even more lightly than the first time. She emits a sharp cry, so muted that I am not certain I have heard it. This is the moment we love, we hunters, when we lift the rifle and the beast seems to hear the fatal shot.

Bring her down now, or let her go? I hesitate. Absolute power. Gently, I press my lips to her neck.

"Don't worry, Madame Saint-Pierre, I'll tell my mother you were here."

She finds the strength to turn the doorknob and leave, moving like a sleepwalker. Slightly hunched, her eyes almost wild, she flees. I watch through the window as she gets into her car. It's obvious she isn't going far.

MY MOTHER COMES in like a gust of wind shortly after the departure of Madame Saint-Pierre. It was a good thing I didn't push things too far.

"Madame Saint-Pierre just left."

"Did you tell her I went to see a sick friend?"

"Yes, Mama."

"Did she wait a long time?"

"Twenty minutes or so."

"Dear God! She's a very busy person, but I couldn't leave Chimène... Do you at least know who she is?"

"Of course... She's the principal of Maryse's school."

"Ah, so you know. I'm astonished. You always seem so... vague about things..."

"I know a lot more than you think, Mama."

"Good. You were polite to her, I hope? She's an important lady. Your father knew how to behave in a lady's presence. He had good manners... I can tell you that! Were you good to her?"

"Yes, Mama."

"You do understand, don't you, Fanfan, that it's thanks to her that your sister is going to that school? It's lucky for us that Maryse is there... Of course, if your father were here it would be different, but he's not here and I have to do the best I can by myself. It's a good thing he bought me this Singer sewing machine, otherwise I don't know what I'd do. Madame Saint-Pierre is a godsend to this house. Your father must have sent her to us. Wherever he is, I'm sure he's looking after us..."

"Is that why you spend all night sewing dresses for Madame Saint-Pierre without being paid a cent...?"

My mother turns angrily to me.

"How do you know that? You mind your own business, young man, if you don't want a couple of good smacks."

Afternoon of a Faun

"But that woman is taking advantage of you, Mama."

"What do you know about life, that you can talk to me like that? If you can't mind your tongue, you can at least wait until you've lost your baby fat before you start having opinions about what goes on in this house. You understand me?"

I stand up to be closer to the door, ready to take off in case there's an explosion. Normally, my mother is a calm person, but she can fly into unpredictable rages at times.

"I'm only saying what I see, Mama. That woman takes advantage of you."

"Without Madame Saint-Pierre, Maryse would not be going to that school."

"I don't see how that school's any better than the lycée. Either way she'll get through her finals with her eyes closed."

"Who's talking about finals?" my mother shouts. "I'm talking about the kind of people she meets at that school, thanks to Madame Saint-Pierre. And if I choose to do her a few favours..."

"But Mama..."

"This discussion is over!"

She comes towards me. A little slip of a woman (my mother is much smaller than I am), she still intimidates me more than anyone else I know. I've never met anyone with more strength of character, or more courage.

"If I have to kill myself on that sewing machine, you two are going to graduate from good schools. As your father wanted you to."

She looks me straight in the eye as she speaks. Her eyes are smouldering. Madame Saint-Pierre is from France, but she came to Port-au-Prince so long ago, before I was born, I think, that by now she seems to have taken on all the cruel customs of Haitian high society. I suppose she might have found it difficult, at the beginning, the way our middle class is so dismissive of those who have no money, no name, no power. But today she's an influential member of the golden circle. In any case, our system has come down to us from slavery days, when we were a colony. That's why certain Europeans slide so easily into the Haitian mud. I know that because I never skipped a single class given by my history teacher, Mr. Zamor, whose vocabulary is so colourful, and the tone of his voice so impassioned, that his is the only course I ever stuck out from beginning to end. It's true, though, that I've always been fascinated by social interactions. Power, money and sex, as my history teacher would say; that's the infernal trinity that drives all men. When you understand that, gentlemen, you understand everything. Love, you ask? he booms in his thunderous voice. Hey, we're only talking about serious things here...

MY SISTER COMES home and installs herself in the easy chair next to the window.

"I'm exhausted," she says, staring up at the ceiling.

"Go take a shower, dear," my mother says.

"That won't make my hunger go away."

"You didn't eat there?" I ask her.

"Oh, they offered me all kinds of things, but I told them I wasn't hungry..."

"That's misplaced pride, Maryse. You were there helping them do their homework."

Afternoon of a Faun

"We were working together..."

"Don't give me that, Maryse, you spend all your time helping those people do their homework."

"I'm telling you, we work together."

"Come off it, Maryse, you go there to help them do their homework. You don't even need a teacher to figure out the answers."

"No, but I do need friends."

"If they're such good friends, how come you don't eat with them?"

"Because I don't want them to think I have some ulterior motive in going to see them. Why do you refuse to understand, Fanfan, that these people are simply my classmates? Whether they're rich or poor, friends are friends. And anyway, they've never once made me feel that they're richer than I am. I've even lent money to Marie-Christine."

"It's all show, Maryse. When the fun and games are over, by which I mean when your final exams are done, they'll all go back to their own social class."

She gives me a lingering, sidelong glance.

"That's all you see, isn't it? Sometimes I think you've already gone sour. And I don't understand why you're like that. You don't owe anything to anyone."

"Let's just say I've never let myself owe anything to anyone."

"But where does it get you, hating people like that?"

"It isn't that... What are you talking about? You sound like someone else when you talk like that."

"What is it, then?" she says sharply, with her patented frown of disdain.

"I simply want to know what kind of world I live in, Maryse. I want to know how it works... I'm sure there's a trick to it, and I want to know what it is. That's all."

My mother comes into the room with a huge bowl of cornmeal mush and a large slice of avocado, which she sets on the table after pushing back piles of catalogues and bits of cloth.

"Mama, why do you choose to pay such a high rent that we're practically starving to death instead of moving to Tiremasse Street, where we could maybe save a bit of money?"

"Who lives on Tiremasse?" my mother says disdainfully. "Listen, Fanfan, if I ever move even one rung down the ladder, I'd get no more clients. Do you think my customers would follow me into that dangerous part of town? They wouldn't even go to Magloire Ambroise Avenue. They're too worried about their cars. And there's all that garbage on the street, and the mud, and the sickening smell... What kind of customers would I have then? Tell me. The kind who would want me make them a blouse for eight gourdes, that's who. Besides, your father wouldn't want us to live there..."

"My father is dead, mama."

"He'll be dead when I say he's dead," she shoots back, turning sharply towards me.

"Maybe I could find a job, Mama."

"No, you are not going to work. You are going to go to law school, like your father wanted."

"But Mama, my father is my father, and I am me... That makes two people."

She looks fixedly at me as though she can see something or someone behind me.

Afternoon of a Faun

"You sound exactly like him," she says, her voice drawn.

"All right, you win. I'm going out."

"Where are you going?" she asks, worried.

"To the Rex Café."

"Will you be home late? The dogs are out in the streets these days."

"I'm not afraid of the *tontons-macoutes*. It's them who're afraid of me."

"Be careful, Fanfan!"

"Oh, he's just teasing you. Let him go, Mama," my sister says, giving me a conspiratorial wink. "It'll be better here with just us two women."

Give me some air!

I DROP IN on Gérard, the museum guard, who owes me money. There are still a few people hanging around the main room. I've never been able to understand what makes people want to spend hours looking at bits of painted cloth hanging on a white wall. It would take me five minutes, if that. These people must have nothing else to do. I know life can be depressing at times, but not that depressing...

Chico motions for me to join him at the Rex. I cross the street in the direction of the café. People pass me without seeing me. In a hurry to get home. What for? I'd rather die than live such a shitty life. Going nowhere. Totally inert. I go into the Rex Café. The old Hindu is still behind the counter. He'll die behind that counter. I order two hamburgers and a glass of pomegranate juice. I'm down to my last three gourdes. Chico also orders a glass of juice. Broke again.

"Simone was here a minute ago. She just left."

I shrug.

"How do you do it?" Chico asks me. "Get women to fall for you like that? It's unbelievable! She was barely able to sit still. I've known Simone for a long time, and I've never seen her like this before... She just met you last week, and she's acting like a drug addict who can't get a fix. Tell me your secret, master, I'll do whatever you ask..."

Laughter.

"You really want to know?"

"I do."

"Your problem, Chico, is that you talk too much."

"What? What am I supposed to do, take off my clothes, maybe?"

"Keep your mouth shut."

"But Fanfan, if I stop talking, she'll leave."

"You don't know that if you haven't tried."

"It seems too risky to me."

"She'll be quiet for a moment, and if she sees that you aren't getting up to leave then she'll start talking... As long as she opens her mouth first, then half your job is done."

"I know myself, Fanfan. She'll take off the minute I stop talking."

"You're right."

He gives me a stunned look.

"Is that all you can think of to tell me?"

"Listen, Chico, to each his own. You, you're not a lover, you're a friend. A confidant. Women like talking to you. You make them feel better. Sometimes I even envy you."

Afternoon of a Faun

"You're making fun of me, you bastard."

"You're right. Let's go to Denz's to listen to music."

DENZ ALWAYS HAS something new to listen to. He's just received an album by Volo Volo, a new group based in Boston. They really did a good job on it—each cut goes somewhere different. I think they're as good as Tabou, but as far as Denz is concerned, Tabou is still Tabou.

"Look, Fanfan, I admit this is a good album, maybe even a great album, but Tabou has put out a dozen albums that are just as good. It's always the same with you: whenever a new act comes down, you get as het up as a flea on a hot rock. Relax, man."

Denz is a bit older than Chico and me. We call him the Godfather. He loves Marlon Brando. He's seen the Coppola film at least a dozen times. But it's only the music that interests him. He hardly ever leaves his place. Doors and windows shut. He spends his days listening to music in the dark. People (mostly musicians) come to him from all over. Sometimes girls from Pétionville come as well. Everyone thinks he's a genius. It doesn't seem to bother him much. As long as he can listen to his music without too much interference.

"Look, Fanfan, I've listened to this album more than a dozen times, and, like I say, it's very good, but before I can say that they really have guts I'll wait until they've put out at least a half-dozen albums. You see, for me it's endurance that counts."

There's a knock on the door. Denz goes to open it.

"Hey, Denz!"

It's Simone. She comes straight in without even looking at me.

"Denz, can I talk to you?" she says, moving towards the small room at the back.

Denz mimes to us that he has no idea what she wants, but he follows her anyway. They stay in the room for a good twenty minutes. Finally Denz comes back in time for the final cut of the Volo Volo.

"Look, Fanfan, it's up to you to solve the problem."

"What's happening?"

"It seems that Minouche went to Simone's place and tore a strip off her. I get the impression that it has something to do with you. Go in and see her, she's waiting for you."

"It's just show, Denz. Simone is yanking your chain."

Denz shrugs his shoulders.

"I don't know anything about women, you know? Go tell her what happened and let me listen to my music. I'd like to see how you get out of this one, anyway, just out of curiosity."

"Denz, Fanfan couldn't care less," Chico puts in. "He even enjoys seeing women fight over him."

"Chico! Chico!"

Simone is calling him from the back room. Chico gets up quickly. I suspect he falls in love with all the women I get mixed up with. He goes into the room and comes out right away.

"She wants to see you."

"Why didn't she call me herself? She called Denz. She called you. I'm not going in if she doesn't call me."

Afternoon of a Faun

"She can't bring herself to say your name out loud. I think she's afraid of something... Isn't that what you wanted?"

"Go fuck yourself, Chico," I say, standing up.

She is sitting at the back of the room.

"What's the matter, Simone?"

She keeps her head down.

"If you don't answer, I'll leave."

She looks up. Eyes filled with tears.

"Why did you leave me?"

"Where did you get that idea? I saw you on Monday."

"Monday! Don't you feel like an eternity has gone by since then?"

"It's only Thursday, Simone. It's only three days, not even that..."

"That's three days when I don't know where I am or who I am or what I'm supposed to do."

"You went to school, though?"

"No."

She looks me straight in the eye. Her face a blank.

"Can I see you?"

"I'm right here, Simone."

"Not here."

"Why not?"

She looks down.

"I want you, Fanfan, I want to be alone with you for a little while. I'd like you to be just with me, just for an hour... Is that too much to ask?"

"No, but it'll have to be here."

So I stay with her for an hour in that little room. She never stops crying, and holding my hand tightly. Every so often she leans her head on my shoulder while rubbing the palm of my left hand. Then suddenly she rears back and stares at me as if seeing me for the first time. Then she kisses my ear. That's her idea of happiness. And then Chico takes her home. I can only guess what they talked about along the way.

MY MOTHER IS busy sewing in the middle of the night.

"You should get some sleep, Mama."

"No, dear, I have to finish this dress. Madame Saint-Pierre is coming to pick it up tomorrow."

I fall asleep to the regular rhythm of the sewing machine. As usual, for that matter.

I'M STILL IN my room, lying on my narrow cot, reading a book about jazz that Denz lent me, when Madame Saint-Pierre arrives.

"Oh, Madeleine! You've finished it already."

"I worked on it all night," my mother says humbly.

"I'm so sorry. You shouldn't have. You must be dead tired now."

"I always work like this... I have two growing children who are very dear to me and I have to bring them up myself."

"I know. Maryse is with us. She has a rare intelligence. Oh, what a beautiful dress! You are truly a matchless marvel, my dear..."

"But you haven't tried it on yet."

Afternoon of a Faun

"I trust you, Madeleine, I'm sure it will make me look ravishing."

I listen to this chit-chat from my bed, feeling distraught.

"Can I speak to you a moment, Madeleine?" Madame Saint-Pierre suddenly says, her voice becoming almost hoarse.

"Of course..."

I take all of this in with a growing sense of unease. Maybe I went too far, and she's going to complain to my mother about me. In which case I'd have about two seconds to get dressed and dash out the back door that opens onto the court-yard. My mother would never forgive me if she lost Madame Saint-Pierre's friendship, even if she does know that it's nothing but a superficial relationship. As far as my mother is concerned, Madame Saint-Pierre holds Maryse's future in the palm of her hand. Damn! What the hell was I thinking, taking such a huge risk? I can get what I want from Simone, or Minouche. But Madame Saint-Pierre is such a mature woman. She's one of the Pétionville bourgeoisie. At the time she might have been impressed by my behaviour, but when she got home, when she'd had time to think about it for a while, she must have realized she'd been had by an impertinent little shit-head. Which is what I am! Damn! Damn! Damn! And damn! The trap is closing in around me. I'm going to have to leave my cosy little nest and forage for myself in the urban jungle. And I have no idea when I'll be able to come back home. My mother is going to want my balls for bookends. Madame Saint-Pierre will no doubt find some excuse to kick Maryse out of her school. All those long nights my mother spent hunched over her sewing machine, for nothing. What an asshole I am. Totally. Barely ten minutes ago I was lying here, minding my own business, thinking I should get up and have some lunch, it was almost eleven o'clock, the time I usually get up on Saturdays, and now here I am little better than a mangy mutt. Damn! Where the hell did my bloody pants get to?

"What is it you want to tell me, Madame Saint-Pierre?"

"I don't know if this will shock you or not, but I want a short dress."

"How short?"

"Above the knee. I want to have my hair cut short, too... What do you think, Madeleine?"

"I think it's good to change your style once in a while."

"It's the first time... I don't know what's come over me. I feel like a giddy schoolgirl..."

Madame Saint-Pierre's joyous laughter, followed by a long silence.

For my part, I've heard enough. I'm already dressed, and without making a sound I slip out the back door.

A FEW HOURS LATER, at the Rex, I'm listening with one ear to Minouche's carrying on.

"The next time I run into that hussy I'm going to scratch her eyes out, take it from me!"

"What have you got against Simone?"

"She's a little snob, that's what... She thinks she's an intellectual because she's read three books. The slut! I know what I'll do, I'll tear her clothes off her back in front of everyone. But she might like that, come to think of it, the little lesbian."

Afternoon of a Faun

"Will you please stop with the gratuitous vulgarity, Minouche? You're not impressing anyone."

"Listen, Fanfan, you know what I'm like; I haven't changed..."

"You're getting upset about nothing."

"What do you mean, nothing? That bitch came to my house and started screaming at me. It's lucky for her I wasn't home; I'd have torn the tongue right out of her head!"

"Finish your hamburger. Anyway, it was you who went to her house."

"Where do you get off, talking to me like that? Are you sleeping with her? What am I saying? Of course you're sleeping with her... So what's new, you sleep with everyone. Have you tried doing it with animals? I'd be surprised if..."

"Stop it, Minouche! Ah, here's Chico..."

"Oh, him! I can't stand him, with his weasel's face... He's only after one thing..."

"Careful, he's a friend."

"A friend!" Minouche says with disdain. "All he wants is for you to pass on your girlfriends when you're done with them. He's like a dog waiting for his master to toss him a bone. Deep down, what he really wants is for you to fuck him in the ass."

"You don't mince words, do you?"

"I call a spade a spade."

Chico comes and sits at our table.

"Hello, Minouche," he says, all smiles.

Without unclenching her teeth, Minouche picks up her math book and leaves.

"Anyone'd think she hates your guts."

"What's up with her?" Chico asks, not attaching much importance to the question.

"She's pissed off because Simone is a classier chick than she is, that's all."

"Right. I'm going to Torgeau to see my uncle, who promised to give me some money. Want to come?"

"I don't want to climb the hill up to Torgeau for a measly five gourdes."

"No," says Chico, laughing. "He's not like the others, he's a generous guy. He's my mother's younger brother. He works for Téléco."

"I didn't ask for his CV, Chico... How much do you think he'll fork out?"

"At least twenty gourdes, maybe more..."

"Well, then, let's go..."

SUDDENLY, JUST AFTER the Au Beurre Chaud bakery:

"That's strange," Chico says. "That's the third time that car has passed us in less than five minutes."

"I didn't notice."

The Mercedes pulls over a little farther on.

"I'm going to check it out," Chico offers.

"Leave it, Chico, I'll go... I know who it is... I'll meet you tonight at the Rex Café."

"All right... You know," he adds, "one day you're going to read about yourself in history books."

"At the Rex, about eight o'clock."

"Ciao!" Chico calls before turning the corner.

Afternoon of a Faun

I get into the car, a new Mercedes that is practically running on its hubcaps. We take the road to Pétionville. She's a good driver (black driving gloves), but I can tell she's nervous. The vein in her right temple. Not a word. Jaws clamped tight. The car is smooth on the rough road. She drives straight down the centre of it. Everything is clean, quiet, luxurious. A hint of perfume. What a class act! She looks straight ahead. Think it'll rain? It's already drizzling. A myriad of tiny sprinkles are hitting the windshield. Without letting her see me I check the car out, at least as much as I can without turning my head. What do I see? An ant going for a quiet stroll on the dashboard. It passes in front of me. I reach out and crush it. No witnesses. Calmly, I watch the countryside go by: houses, people, trees. We arrive in Pétionville. The road is a bit wet and quite steep in certain places, but the car is so comfortable I never feel we're in danger. Flat calm. So happy to be in this heap that I almost forget about Madame Saint-Pierre sitting beside me. Still nervous. Then we're at Kenscoff, in the heights of Pétionville, high above the heat of Port-au-Prince. Where the air is purer. Switzerland without the snow. I feel like I'm a million miles away. In another world. A world gained neither by work nor study. Not even by money. Anyone living up here has put a wall between themselves and the new. Their only enemy is overpopulation. And the mountain is their ultimate refuge. The car makes a quick left turn onto a hilly road that soon gives onto a dirt lane. No house in sight. Perfect place for a crime. The car is now completely stopped, but Madame Saint-Pierre keeps her hands clenched on the steering wheel. I watch her from the corner of my eye. She starts to speak, then checks herself at the last second. Her chin points towards the sky, already sprinkled with stars so low I feel I could reach out and grab a cluster of them in my hand. Madame Saint-Pierre's worried brow. Twin creases at the corners of her mouth. I sit motionless, waiting. Time is on my side. Suddenly, Madame Saint-Pierre's look becomes almost clouded. Her breathing quickens. She tries to calm herself by flattening her hands against the wheel.

"I don't want..."

Her face is closing down now.

"For one thing, you could be my son..."

Another pause, this one shorter.

"That's it: you could be my son," she says, as though she has made a decision.

She turns towards me. An infinitely gentle look. Like a plea.

"And so?" I say, my voice even.

"And so..."

She doesn't finish the sentence. Her head must be on fire. She lowers her eyes, then slowly raises her head. Her mass of thick hair changes sides. There is an expression of perfect astonishment on her face. A wounded beast who doesn't even know where she's been hit. In her womb? In her heart?

"I don't want to," she says, a whisper.

I slide as far away from her as I can get, pushing myself up against the passenger door. She thinks I'm trying to get away. Mild panic in her eyes. Is she frightening me? Her eyes question me mutely. Is it her age? Her scent? Do her hands disgust me? She doesn't understand why I don't want to take her. She must give herself. Suddenly I've turned the tables. Now I'm the prey. She leans towards me. Hesitant. Her upper body turned in my direction. And slowly she unbuttons her blouse. Her eyes sparkle in the darkness. There is a full moon. She touches me with the tips of her fingers, as though I were a holy relic. Then with her mouth. I relax into it. She licks me with the tip of her tongue. Like she wants to taste me. The salt of my skin. Then with her lips. Her huge, carnivorous mouth. My body is slick with her saliva. A pulling back. A throaty cry. A mouth twisted with desire too long held back. I hear nothing but cries, chuckles, whimperings. A curious lexicon of onomatopoeias, interjections, borborygmi. Then the keening of a wounded beast. Interminable even as it peaks. And down she comes.

Ten minutes later.

"My God!" she breathes. "What was that?"

THE DRIVE BACK seems much shorter. Not a word has been spoken in the car. Me, silent as always. Her head in some world to which I have no access. Even with the tumult raging inside her she retains a certain elegant air. I slide my eyes sideways to take in her long, thoroughbred's legs. When we leave Pétionville she says, simply:

"If Madeleine learns about this she'll never forgive me."

I say nothing. I get the impression she is not trying to dissuade me from telling my mother about us. Something like that.

She seems to me to be a courageous woman, able to face up to her responsibilities. Maybe she just wants me to know that whatever wrong has been done has been done by her. Poor Madame Saint-Pierre.

. She doesn't realize how the city has changed.

"Where do you want me to drop you off?" she asks in a very sweet, almost submissive tone of voice.

"At the Rex Café."

"I saw you there yesterday afternoon."

The car makes a left turn, cruises the length of National Palace and turns onto Capois Street, then makes a right and comes to a stop in front of the Rex.

"Goodbye, Madame Saint-Pierre."

"Can't you call me Françoise?... It would please me so much..."

I open the door. She grabs my arm and turns my face towards hers, gives me a long kiss.

"Would you like it if I cut my hair short?"

An anxious tic at the corner of her mouth.

"Yes," I say.

She smiles. I manage to get out of the car, and it pulls away.

I GO INTO the bar. Chico is sitting by himself in a corner, flipping through the pages of a magazine. I make my way towards him. He looks up just as I get there.

"Fucked. My uncle wasn't there. Of all the rotten luck! What about you? How did you get on with your bourgeoise?"

"Next time I'm going to make her pay me."

"Good," Chico says calmly. "I'll be able to get some new shoes."

Afternoon of a Faun

More customers arrive. The nine o'clock crowd is leaving the Rex Theatre, next door. There's a new song on the radio.

"I don't get people like that," says Chico. "He seemed like a nice guy..."

The announcer has just said the singer's name: Dodo.

"Dodo! I don't know any Dodo. Where's he from, I wonder?"

"For sure Denz would know."

"Not me. I'm going home."

Even Nice Girls Do It

AT THE LAST MINUTE, Christina changes her mind and decides to stay home and rest. She hasn't felt well all afternoon. She knows she's probably only coming down with the flu, but she doesn't want to go out feeling like this. She feels cold deep down into her bones (and she's in a tropical country). Ever since she arrived in Port-au-Prince, her greatest fear has been contracting malaria. She knows what she's going to do. She's going to make herself a nice hot toddy (rum, lemon, sugar) and curl up in bed with the new John le Carré. She likes his dry, refined sense of humour. This is how she intends to spend the evening. Harry can go to the Widmaiers' without her.

"You're sure you don't mind if I don't go, sweetie?"

"I'd rather you came with me, but if you're not feeling well, my dear . . . I'll just show up for form's sake and come home as soon as possible."

She knows Harry has no intention of leaving the party until the "last interesting woman" has departed, which means the woman with the roundest ass and the thickest lips. Suffice to say that Harry has a weakness for the young Haitian women who invariably show up at the Widmaiers' parties. But Christina is not a jealous woman, and Harry isn't a fool. He likes coming home. If he fantasizes about black women that's his business. In a way, it has nothing to do with her. Christina, it should be pointed out, is a brunette, born to New York Jewish parents. She loves Woody Allen, and her favourite writer (apart from le Carré) is Philip Roth. Which means she appreciates humour and cultivates an air of desperation towards life. She has followed Harry here and has landed a job teaching contemporary literature at the Union School. Harry works at the American Embassy as the cultural attaché. He's the lean type (but well muscled) with a prominent brow, which makes him look vaguely like a serial killer. His eyes, however, are bright, and he has the lips of a gourmand. He's difficult to define. As for Christina, she's a tad on the dry side, thin-lipped, tight-bummed, but very intelligent and a veritable dynamo of energy. It amuses her that men find her attractive. At parties she is never at a loss for admirers. But she much prefers intellectual conversation to primitive sex. Which is not easy to explain to a man with a hard-on. And so she avoids the usual parties as much as possible, since they are, let's face it, nothing but pretexts for drinking and cruising. Which became clear the night a drunk pinched June's bottom. June is their seventeen-year-old daughter, born in Manhattan. The name June doesn't suit her. Harry named her after a Henry Miller character he found particularly disturbing. A sort of femme fatale who evoked every hell Miller could concoct. And every paradise. Harry's daughter is nothing like that. She's a classic beauty. Nicely rounded, as the saying sometimes goes. Adored by her professors. So gifted she takes her courses in French—a language she hadn't known before coming to Port-au-Prince—and is doing quite well. She never raises her voice. Always calm. Usually to be found in her room either studying or listening to music. She so seldom goes to her friends' surprise parties at Kenscoff or La Boule that her friends have pretty much taken her off their list. Sometimes Christina wonders, with a growing sense of unease, if her daughter isn't turning into a nun before their very eyes. At first it was a joke that she and Harry shared, but lately it's begun to be a serious concern. To the point where Christina has started to be on the lookout for her daughter.

"June, you'll never guess who I ran into today."

"Hansy."

"How did you know?"

"I know you, mother. You've been talking about him for a week. I knew you'd hook up with him sooner or later."

Christina takes a shallow breath.

"Do you mind that I invited him over next Saturday for a little badminton party?"

"I have an exam on Monday."

"But my dear, you study all the time. You should get some exercise."

"But mother, we do all kinds of sports at school."

"My dear, there's more to life than sports," Christina says, sounding slightly vexed. "There are boys, too, and they're good for our equilibrium."

Even Nice Girls Do It

"What do you mean by that, Mother?"

"June!"

"I'm joking. I know exactly what you mean, Mother, and I assure you I have no problems with my equilibrium."

Christina seems to reflect on this for a moment.

"My dear, you know that the mind isn't everything."

"Why are you telling me this?" asks June, suddenly anxious.

"I'm telling you this," Christina begins, keeping her voice gentle, "because I myself have fallen into this trap."

"I don't get you."

This time Christina takes a deep breath.

"All right... Well, I mean I wasted a lot of chances I might have had with men I found interesting because, to put it simply, I sublimated my intellect as an adolescent."

"You know, I don't always follow you, mother."

"Good God!... Listen, sweetie, there are times when the body must speak out... No other part of you... just the body... Nothing you can do about it. It's the way we're made. It's physical, June. It's natural. We're animals, you know, just like other animals. Monkeys do it. Dogs do it. Birds do it. For all I know even plants do it. June... June, look at me... June, your mother does it. Even nice girls do it. Do you understand what I'm saying?"

"Look, Mother, I'm not stupid. I know all about that."

"June, there's a huge difference between knowing something and accepting it. Or rather experiencing it. I'd hate to see you going down the same path I took. I have suffered too much, and I want to save you from the same suffering before it's too late... I don't want you to become nothing but an intellectual. I want you to have a good mind, of course I do, but I also want you to have... a body. Do you see what I mean?"

"Yes, Mother."

THEY TALKED FOR a while longer, and then June went up to her room to work on an assignment. Christina took a long, cold shower (menopause). Then she called her best friend, Françoise (she'd met Françoise Saint-Pierre shortly after her arrival in Port-au-Prince). For a brief time, Françoise had been Harry's mistress (Christina knows that), but he dropped her when he started becoming interested in Haitian women.

"Françoise, I told her everything... Absolutely everything, including the bit about animals. I felt like a complete nincompoop! She listened calmly enough, as she always does, but I know her, I know she was shaken... Of course she was, she had to have been, seventeen years old, beautiful as she is, and not a soul calling her at home except when they need help with their homework... Do you think that's normal? What would you have me do? I had to take the bull by the horns! Now all I can do is wait and see... Yes, Françoise, wait. I've planted the seed, now I wait for it to bear fruit... Of course I'm worried, what do you think? She might decide to go out with four different boys at the same time. But I'd prefer that! I can't sleep. All I hear is the time bomb ticking, and I try to guess when the damn thing is going to go off! You know, I see her when she's a young woman indulging in fantasies in her bedroom. No, no, she has to get out, get some fresh air, meet some young men, enjoy herself, have fun, you know what I mean, it's important for her to do that! Life is too absurd, Françoise, to be taken so seriously. I want her to let herself go (Christina begins to cry), get some kicks, be happy, enjoy life, gobble up everything that love has to offer (she sobs). That's all I want for her. Go ahead and say it, all the things that I never had... Yes, I know one can't make up for what's missing in one's own life by vicariously living another person's life... Oh, I've got to go, Harry's just come home. As far as he's concerned, everything's just ducky... Lots of sun, tropical fruit, Haitian women with big asses: he thinks he's died and gone to heaven. And there are no problems in paradise... I'll call you later... And what about you, anything good going on with you these days, Françoise?"

A long pause.

"Let's get together soon and talk about it..."

"My dear, you're leaving me on tenterhooks..."

"I'll call you when we have more time to..."

"How about tomorrow, at the Bellevue... Harry has a tennis match... We can have lunch together."

"Great."

"I can't wait to hear all about it, Françoise. Really."

THAT CONVERSATION took place exactly one week ago. Today, Christina feels a fever coming on, and she's mentally preparing herself for a restful evening with a good rum punch and a good read, followed by a good sleep. At the last minute she decides not to go to her own bedroom, but goes instead into the guest room. It's a pretty room, much smaller than the master bedroom, but well appointed and extremely comfortable. Christina likes taking refuge in this room because it reminds her of her university days, when she lived in a rooming house not far from Columbia U. She felt torn, at the time, between solitude and freedom. Or rather, she felt more at loose ends than free. She spent her time reading Virginia Woolf (even though she did her dissertation on Colette) hoping someone would come and knock on her door. Now she reads nothing but mystery novels or the latest Philip Roth (luckily he publishes about a book a year) to try to pamper the migraine that never gives her a minute's rest. In any case, this room makes her feel like the free, young, solitary woman she was in the early 1960s. The guest room opens onto the verandah, where Absalom sleeps when Harry isn't in the house. Absalom is the young man recommended to them by the Widmaiers. A total pearl, according to Jacqueline Widmaier. Polite, a good worker and above all intelligent. Sometimes Christina thinks about bringing him to New York when Harry's posting is finished. He already speaks a bit of rudimentary English and understands everything anyone says to him. Harry is very fond of him because of his quick wit. The speed at which he grasps the most complex situations never ceases to amaze them. Absalom is already getting himself ready for bed. He has a room at the far end of the courtyard where he keeps his things, but Harry has asked him to sleep on the verandah when he has to come home late after a party, or after spending a torrid night with one of his Annaïses. That way Absalom can respond quickly to the slightest alarm. There are assassins and thieves everywhere these days. Christina smiles at the thought that no one knows she is here, because she decided only at the last minute not to go to the party. She hears June going down the stairs to get herself a glass of milk in the kitchen. She hears her daughter's footsteps going back up the well-waxed stairs. Odd, she thinks, smiling, how clearly one can hear everything that goes on in the house from this little room. She'd never noticed it before. It's like an acoustic trap. Through the half-opened window she can follow Absalom's slightest movement on the verandah. In her room, June is listening to the Billie Holiday album they gave her for her seventeenth birthday. What a smart girl she is! she thinks, if a bit inscrutable at times. An Oriental calm. A steady flame in the eye of the storm. Christina pictures her daughter sitting in her room listening to the record and trying to decode the dazzling poetry in Billie Holiday's songs of despair and longing. Absalom is also listening to music on a tiny radio he keeps beside his head. Haitian music. Very sensual, joyous, lively. Music made to dance to. Haitian music and painting took Christina's breath away when she first came to Port-au-Prince. So different from the miserable lives the people here live. They may be starving, but they go on creating this joyous music, these fantastically colourful paintings, so filled with life. We Americans, on the other hand, who have everything, spend all our time moaning and groaning. Pessimism. The Haitian is the absolute opposite, she thinks, of the New York Jew. The Jew according to Woody Allen and Philip Roth. Modern America is like a fast-food restaurant serving up despair. Man cannot live on hamburgers alone, says the Bible. One (Woody Allen) brings out a film a year. The other (Philip Roth), a book. Our annual ration of angst. American angst. The starving poor. The despairing rich. But here we're a long way from Manhattan. Despite its terrible misery, Christina recalls (with a rueful smile) how much she missed Manhattan when she first came to Haiti. Manhattan snobbery runs in her veins. The radical chic of the sixties, that was her era. The bright lights, the drive-by murders, the Yellow Cabs, the wet sidewalks, Cuban coffee, the happy hookers. Life in the fast lane, what could she say! At first she missed it all. Not so much, now. She remembers with an enigmatic smile that she could do up there in one day what it takes her six months to accomplish here.

"Where does the time go?" she asks herself, without trying to find an answer.

SHE WAS SO caught up in these thoughts that she hadn't noticed a curious exchange taking place out on the verandah.

She listens.

"No, Miss June, I don't want to lose my work. We can't do this . . . If Madame finds out, she'll send me packing . . ."

"There's no one here," June says dryly.

Christina is already bathed in sweat. June, her daughter, is forcing herself on a man. On their servant. Christina crawls across the floor to the window. Slowly, without making a sound, she raises her body. Cocks her head. Finally, she sees Absalom. He is lying on his back, and June is sitting astride him. A slight wind stirs the leaves of the magnifi-

Even Nice Girls Do It

cent tree that completely hides the verandah from the view of the neighbours.

Calmly, June removes her blouse. Absalom keeps his eyes tightly shut. June's firm breasts. Their rosy tips: erect and stiff. Christina feels her skin prickling. With a shiver she thinks: "My daughter is in heat." And she watches, fascinated. The whole game in slow motion. Time slackened. The terrific concentration in her face. June, her June, is coolly pulling Absalom's trousers down to his knees. Now there she is avidly seizing his white-hot penis and sliding it peremptorily under her skirt. At the moment of contact she briefly closes her eyes. Her red tongue comes out to moisten her lips. And she settles herself astride Absalom, hard, without a sound. Time suspended. Her nostrils flare and contract, flare and contract, quicker and quicker. Time halted. And then the orgasm. Brutal. Christina watches her daughter's pleasure, hears her squealing like a mouse caught in a trap. It seems to go on interminably. And at the precise moment when it appears to be over, it takes on new life. She comes again. An invisible bird calls from the leaves of the mango tree. June is riding Absalom like a stallion, galloping him. She comes again, her mouth open this time. She howls. A sound that could be either pleasure or pain. And again it starts. Desire seems to have given her fresh energy. An animal trying to bite her own tail. Desire at fever pitch. A strident cry, as though she wants it to end but can't bring herself to stop. She is galloping, faster and faster. Higher and higher. For a fraction of a second Christina sees her pubic mound. Beads of sweat on her worried brow. Her serious little girl. Her lips parted as though she is making a tender and prolonged recitation. As though she is praying. Christina is crying softly. This life (Absalom's penis) thrust into her daughter's belly. A few jerking movements. She rears. Her breasts point to heaven. Mouth twisted. Long groans. She wants to shed her skin. The pain. More spasms. And everything stops. Her body lying stretched out on Absalom's. Resting. An occasional shudder. Like a fish out of water. And then, with a sound like that of a marine mammal, her body begins to move again. Gently. This intolerable gentleness. Suddenly her eyes open wide, like those of someone waking up from a terrible nightmare. More sharp groans. And then she is screaming. Her body stiffens into a perfect arc. The veins stand out on her neck. "She's going to hurt herself," Christina suddenly thinks. But on her face there appears a pleasure so intense, so violent, so naked, that Christina lowers her eyes. A private moment. "I've never known anything like that," she says to herself, sliding to the floor. She lies there crying for so long she eventually falls asleep, curled up in the fetal position.

Christina is startled awake when she hears Harry's car in the drive. Her immediate thought is that Harry must on no account find June in such a position. She tries to calm herself enough to risk raising her head to look out the window. No one there. It's as though nothing has happened. She hears Harry climbing the stairs. And Billie Holiday's passionate voice ("Strange Fruit") coming once again from June's bedroom.

Even Nice Girls Do It

Woman of Prey

THIS MORNING I have to go meet a young musician at his house. He's seventeen (same litter as me) and has just put out his first album. Denz asked me to check him out. He wants to work with him. He must be good if Denz is taking such an early interest in him. Usually Denz waits until someone has two or three albums out before he bothers to consider them anything more than a greenhorn. I've also read about him in the media. According to the influential music critic Gérald Merceron, who is also a good friend of Denz's, by the way, this Jude Michel dude is the most original lyricist to have appeared on the scene in the past thirty years, by a long shot. Say since Ti Paris (the alcoholic bard). No one knows hardly anything about him except that his mother died of uterine cancer when he was six, and he never knew his father. He lives with his old aunt in Poste-Marchand, one of the more populous quarters in Port-au-Prince.

"Excuse me, sir, but I've been wandering around in this area for a half an hour now, and . . ."

"I know," the man says grumpily. "This is the sixth time you've passed in front of my door."

"I'm looking for a guy named Jude Michel... Do you know him?"

"No... I don't know any Jude Michel."

"He's a young musician..."

"Ah, you mean Dodo, Sylvana's nephew... What's he done? I know his aunt, she's a respectable lady..."

"He's just put out a fine first album."

"Ah, that good-for-nothing... Now that Sylvana's sick and can't take care of him anymore, he's going to go to the dogs. He never did want to stay in school. Sylvana sent him to J.B. Damien to learn a trade, and do you think he was able to stick it out for a single course? Do you know what lengths that woman had to go to to get him admitted into that school? They only take a few students every year, but it's an excellent school. I got a nephew went to it, and he's doing pretty well for himself today."

"I gather his mother is dead," I say, taking out my notebook.

"Forget it!" he says, contempt in his voice. "I don't talk to cops or journalists."

"I'm just doing some research for a history paper."

"Ah, well, how would I know? Still, I don't like people writing down what I say..."

I put my notebook back in my pocket.

"That's more like it... He's Lumane's son, Sylvana's little sister... She was a fine singer, but she died in the darkest misery you can imagine. And so when Dodo started showing an interest in music, Sylvana did everything she could to keep him away from it..."

"What kind of guy is he?"

Woman of Prey

The man seems taken aback by the question.

"He's a fine, upstanding young man, but like I said, that's no way to make a living." He pauses. "At least, not in Haiti."

"Do you know what they said about him in *Le Nouvelliste* the other day?"

"No, I don't," the man says dryly. "I don't read the paper."

"They said he was the most original musician to come along in thirty years. You have to go all the way back to Ti Paris..."

"Ah! Ti Paris...I like Ti Paris. He's a real song-man. He didn't give a damn about nothing, except music. Music was his whole life. His songs go right to my heart...I remember he said in one of his songs that he was always drunk, ("Ev'ry day I drinks away"), which is not a word of a lie, I know that for a fact."

"You knew him well, then?"

His face takes on a nostalgic look.

"For sure I knew him. In them days we used to go to the same joint: Chez la Mère Jeanne. Oh boy, the food was terrible there. But there was this young waitress, firm breasts, a real saucy one, she was, but beautiful, beautiful, my friend."

He spends some time thinking about her.

"I even think...I'm not sure...but I think she had a kid by Ti Paris...That Ti Paris, he had eleven kids by seven different women. He loved women, and they returned the favour... That was his downfall, I guess...Them three things always go together: women, music and booze..."

"What about you?"

"What do you mean?"

41

"Haven't you done a few things you regret in your life?"

The man looks me in the eye like someone on the verge of making a terrible confession, but then he draws back.

"Who hasn't? That's all I've got to say..."

"Jude Michel's address... A friend of mine wants to work with him."

"Work? Dodo doesn't know the meaning of the word... Scratching away on a guitar, I don't call that work... All right, go down to the crossroads, then turn left and keep going right to the end of the dirt lane..."

"And then?"

"Then you're there. You can't miss it."

A TALL, THIN young man opens the door and shows me into a tiny, overheated room. An old guitar on the table.

"I guess I'm not the first journalist"—I decided to pass myself off as a journalist—"to come here to waste your time..."

A candid smile flutters across his sensual lips.

"You're the first and will probably be the only."

"But you got such a great write-up by Gérald Merceron in last weekend's paper."

"Monsieur Merceron showed it to me before it came out. I was pretty happy with it..."

"Ah, so you know him?"

"He gave me a lot of advice when I was putting the album together."

"So how do you feel?"

"Sad..."

"Oh, yeah? Why's that?"

Woman of Prey

"I don't know. I didn't get a wink of sleep last night... My heart was pounding like anything."

"And you have no idea why?"

"To tell you the truth, no."

"It's always like that when something important happens," says a calm voice from somewhere behind me.

I turn around a bit quickly. A very elegant lady is sitting in a dark corner of the room. Huge eyes, refined hands, the same age as Madame Saint-Pierre. She opens her Gucci handbag (the famous golden G) and takes out a slender cigarette holder.

"I was telling Jude before you arrived not to make such a fuss about it, because it's perfectly normal. It's too much emotion in too little time."

"You're right," I say.

"And of course," she adds in a whisper that contains all the sensuality in the world, "Jude is so young..."

"Excuse me, ma'am, I don't mean to shake you up, but would you mind telling me what you think of his album?"

"What I think of his album?" she says, with a pretty laugh. "Well, I think Jude has a devastating talent."

"Do you have a favourite cut?"

Silence.

"'Crazy About You.'"

"Why's that?"

"I find it orgasmic."

"Ah! And the rest of the disc? What do you think of the musical arrangements? I have a good friend who does arrangements, too..."

"Denz."

"You know him?"

"Of course."

"I don't," says Jude, "but I really like his work."

The woman stands up abruptly.

"Excuse me, but I must go... Jude, I'll come by to pick you up around seven tonight."

A whiff of Nina Ricci.

"WHO WAS THAT?" I ask.

"I don't know..." Jude lets out. "She showed up yesterday morning, and she's been back every two hours since then."

"Do you know what she wants?"

"I don't know that, either..."

"No idea?"

"Well, yeah, but I'm a bit afraid."

"Afraid of what?"

"Of her... I don't know what's happening to me. Barely a week ago I couldn't imagine anything like this, and now, all of a sudden, everyone wants to meet me. But it isn't me who's changed..."

He stops and holds his head in his hands.

"What do you want from me? I can't understand a thing... She's beautiful, rich, she knows everyone, and here I am with nothing. I live in Poste Marchand with an old, sick aunt. I don't know what there is here that a woman like her would find attractive."

"Your talent. There are some women who only get turned on by new talent."

Woman of Prey

"What talent?" he says, banging his head against the wall. "I steal things from here and there: rock, jazz, rara, konpa direct, Spanish music . . . I didn't invent a thing."

"Maybe, but it makes a good sauce."

He stops pacing the floor and stares at me fixedly, his face looking feverish.

"It's funny you should mention sauce. I've always been interested in cooking, but for some reason my aunt has never wanted to teach me."

"But music is a lot like cooking, isn't it, Jude? Oddly enough."

His eyes light up.

"Maybe that's it!" he exclaims. "I like talking to you . . . I don't even know your name . . ."

"Fanfan."

"I didn't sleep all night, Fanfan. Every time I closed my eyes, I saw that woman. I felt like I was caught in a funnel. And now I don't know whether I was dreaming or wide awake."

"You must be tired. I'll leave now so you can get some rest."

"But you came all this way . . ."

"I just came to tell you that Denz would like you to drop by some time."

His face lights up.

"I'd like to meet him. He's been my idol for such a long time. He does cool arrangements," he says with a feeble smile. "It's just that my aunt is sick. I have to look after her."

He takes up his guitar and begins to play one of his tunes, then puts the instrument back on the table.

"She said she'll come back to get me at seven o'clock, about, but I'm sure she'll be back before that. If only I knew for sure what she wanted from me. My head hurts, like someone's been sticking long, thin needles right through my skull... You'll come back? We could talk some more. I feel a connection between us..."

"Yes, I'll come back another time," I say, heading for the door.

As I'm about to go through it I turn and see him already stretched out on his iron cot. On his back, arms crossed over his chest and his mouth sagging open. Exhausted.

Outside, the strong smell of garbage goes right to the back of my throat. I didn't get a good look at the quarter on my way here, so I decide to walk around a bit, taking a different route back. Just after I turn my second corner I see a new Mercedes parked under a tree. It's her! He was right. She shoots me a cold glance, as though she's never seen me before. She has the shut-down look of a bird of prey on the point of making its fatal swoop. Fatal, that is, for the rabbit. The minute I reach the car it begins to roll slowly down to the house of the young musician whose talent the critics have unanimously declared to be the hope of our generation.

Woman of Prey

One Good Deed

CHARLIE QUIT SCHOOL during second term for one very simple reason: he was too beautiful to spend the whole day cooped up in a classroom. Women had been after him for a long time. He was still a virgin when his geography teacher offered him a ride home and then took him to her house instead. Since then, Charlie realized he could get anything he wanted out of women. So what was the use of staying in school when real life was bustling out on the street? The sweet, ripe fruit of the tree of good and evil was dangling inches from his outstretched hand. And Charlie had a good appetite. All the girls adored him except one: his sister, who, curiously, was not particularly gifted by nature. Every time she bragged that she was Charlie's sister, someone would always say: "But how is that possible!" After that, she changed tactics. Now she says: "Charlie may have looks, but I have intelligence." But she might as well save her breath. Sometimes I think it best to just say nothing and give in to your fate. Charlie is beautiful, that's all there is to it. There are those who reveal themselves to be beautiful only after you've looked at them for a certain length of time, and others who, as they say, have beautiful souls. At the risk of repeating myself, Charlie is beautiful, by which I mean that whenever he enters a room, heads turn: women look at him with an avidity bordering on dementia (they literally devour him with their eyes), and men with a certain pique. A truly beautiful man is rarer than you might think. At first it was incredible. Charlie would scoop up any woman who gave him a certain come-hither look (and did they ever really look at him any other way?), so that his miniscule room on Christophe Avenue became a kind of bordello. A new girl would arrive as the previous one was leaving, still fixing her hair. Sometimes they met in his bed. These days, however, he's being more selective. He's been known to turn down a staggering beauty and go home with a woman who is more fun to be with, or who makes him laugh, or even one who is downright ugly but has a certain charm, or an interesting walk, or even one who seems to have accepted the fact that no one will ever be interested in her. When he goes to a disco, no one, not even Charlie himself, has the slightest idea who he's going to leave with.

BEFORE WE GO too much further, you should know that Charlie's parents are poor but respectable. His father threw him out of the house the day he quit school. He went to live with one of his cousins in Carrefour-Feuilles. Said cousin being an Adventist preacher, very strict, who prayed every night at nine o'clock, went to bed at nine-thirty, and didn't let anyone in after ten. After a month of this monastic regime, during which he believed he was going insane, Charlie moved

in with a friend who lives in Pacot. This arrangement didn't
work, either, since the friend's young wife fell for him in a big
way, placing him in an embarrassing situation. He found himself stuck between a benefactor and a woman for whom he felt
no desire whatsoever. One of the cardinal rules in the lover's
social code is: never live under the same roof with a woman
you've turned down. Once again, Charlie had to pack his bags.
Eventually he found the miniscule room on Christophe Avenue, above a shoe store. He'd kept in touch with his mother
and sister, despite their being absolutely forbidden from contact by his father: no members of the family (including uncles,
aunts, and cousins) were allowed to so much as speak to him.
"I have only one child," he was heard to say, watching Rachel do
her homework. Ever since discovering the great injustice done
to her by nature in the matter of aesthetics, she had sought
solace in her studies (it could have been worse: it could have
been religion). But since her brother's banishment, Rachel
has stopped hating him. Especially now that their parents
are getting old. They still work in service for the Abels, a rich
family that owns many houses, including the villa in Bourdon.
Madame Abel picks them up in the morning and brings them
back each evening (a job she never leaves to her driver). Work at
the Abels isn't all that demanding, except for the stairway that
becomes steeper with each passing year. They are good Chris-
tians who treat their domestics charitably. As far as cooking
is concerned, the ambassador (François Abel was the Haitian
ambassador to London during the Second World War) isn't
hard to please. His menu hasn't varied in twenty years, except

that for the past two years he hasn't drunk so much as a glass of water after six o'clock in the evening. What the ambassador brought back with him from London (apart from a box of Cuban cigars given to him by Winston Churchill during an unforgettable meeting) was a sense of discipline, sartorial elegance and a heightened respect for the individual. Charlie's elderly parents are therefore treated with the same respect that the ambassador would accord to his colleagues, astonishing in a country where domestics are often treated like slaves. To Charlie's father, it goes without saying, the ambassador is a living god. Work is evenly divided in the Abel household, where it is believed (as one believes that Jesus is the son of God) that England is the most civilized country on the planet. Charlie's mother works inside (kitchen, cleaning and telephone), while his father looks after things around the yard (garden, garage, raising the gate whenever he expects the ambassador's car to arrive). In this way the peaceful lives of these two couples (masters and domestics) have run for more than twenty years.

CHARLIE KNOWS THAT every Wednesday his father accompanies the ambassador into the city. He takes advantage of his father's absence to spend that day with his mother at the Abels' villa. Even when Charlie and his father were still close, his father never wanted his son to visit the villa, saying that he could not receive him properly in a house in which he was not the master. His mother, on the other hand, has never felt the least bit humiliated by the work she does. So Charlie fell into the habit of visiting his mother on Wednesdays. Sometimes they don't even talk. She'll make him a cup of coffee, which he will sip while she goes on with her housework or prepares the Abels' dinner. This day, he finds his mother sitting at the kitchen table, peeling potatoes.

"Hello, Mama."

She jumps.

"Don't tell me your father left that gate open again. It's the same thing every Wednesday; he gets as excited as a child when he has to go into town with the ambassador…"

"No problem, I closed it… Are you okay, Mama?"

Silence.

"What's the matter, Mama? You don't seem yourself today."

"I'm worried about your father."

"What for? Is he sick?"

Another silence.

"I don't think he's going to be able to resist…"

"Resist what? Now you've got me worried, Mama."

She takes a deep breath.

"You know what a prideful man your father is… Well, here it is: for the past two weeks there's been a young girl living here. The daughter of the ambassador's elder brother, Monsieur Georges, who has just died. Monsieur Georges lived all his life in Paris. He was married there to a Frenchwoman from a noble family… The daughter doesn't want to live with her mother in France, and so she came to live here."

"So, what's wrong with that? The ambassasor's her uncle…"

"Yes, but Monsieur Georges was not like the ambassador. He was, how can I put it, more aristocratic. He was even snootier than his wife, who at least is a real aristocrat. They came here two Christmases ago..."

"Oh, to hell with Georges and his upper-class hussy..."

His mother opens her eyes wide.

"Don't make fun... She's a terror, that girl. This morning she yelled at your father again... And I could see how much effort it took him to keep from putting her in her place. Truly, she treats us like we were a couple of slaves, and the ambasssador..."

"Yes, yes, so why doesn't he just speak to the ambassador? You've always said he was justice incarnate."

"I know, but the ambassador adored his brother, he's the only brother he had, and it makes him very happy to have his brother's daughter living with us... Your father hasn't the heart to tell him what she's like... you understand?

"No, Mama, I'm sorry but I don't understand."

His mother raises a face ravaged by pain.

"He'll never do it, and we'll have to leave the villa."

"You would rather lose this great job than complain about the behaviour of this girl?"

His mother goes back to peeling potatoes, as though she hasn't heard him.

"That's what I said to him, Charles... And he said to me that he'll never speak to the ambassador. And he won't, I know it, and we'll soon have to quit this place."

"Where is this girl?"

"She's probably at the Bellevue Circle playing tennis. It's just across the way."

One Good Deed

"What does she look like?"

"Very pretty... She takes after her mother, but she has the personality of her father... very conscious of what she is..."

"Okay, Mama, I've got to go... Can you lend me a little money?"

"Of course I can, but from now on I'm going to have to watch what I spend... Oh, my God, I don't know what he's going to say to the ambassador to explain why we're leaving... Oh, Charles, what's going to happen to us? We're like one big family here."

"I've got to go now... See you next week."

"Maybe... I don't know. I don't have any control over my life..."

THERE ARE STILL a few people on the courts, despite the oppressive heat.

"Who's that girl, there?" Charlie asks the gardener who is standing beside him.

"Mademoiselle Abel... She just got here... She's a good player, but she's got a lousy personality."

"How do you know that?"

"Ha! When she loses, she shouts insults at everybody, even the umpire."

"I'd like to speak to her."

"Why? You doing something for her?"

"No, I just want to speak to her."

"I doubt that that's possible, my friend."

"We'll see."

THE BAR IS at the far end of the courts.

"Whisky," Charlie says.

The barman looks at him.

"I don't recall seeing you here before."

"It's the first time I've been here . . . and it won't be the last."

"Forgive me, my friend, but I doubt that very much. This is a private club. That's why it's called the Circle, you see? Either you join, or else you have to be invited here by one of the members. Otherwise . . ."

"I see you know the rules pretty well."

The barman smiles.

"I've been working here for twenty years, my friend . . . I not only know all the rules, I know all the people, and I know their ways."

"Well, then, you must know my father."

The barman looks closely at Charlie.

"Your father?"

"No, he's not a member," Charlie says, laughing. "He works across there, at Ambassador Abel's place."

The barman's expansive smile.

"You ask me do I know your father? And how! We started working together. Me, here, him at the ambassador's. How is he doing? I haven't seen him in a while, now. A very upright man, your father. And a good friend . . . In a way, he's just like the ambassador. They're like a couple of twins . . . They come from different social classes, but deep down they're the same kind of person . . . What's up with your father?"

"He's having problems."

"Health, I'd guess."

One Good Deed

"No, thank God, he's all right on that side of things. He's having problems at work."

The barman can hardly restrain a cry of surprise.

"With the ambassador?"

"No, with his niece."

"Mademoiselle Abel," says the barman, dryly. "I can understand that."

"I'd like to meet her..."

"She should be on the court right now... I can tell you, though, she's not an easy one to deal with..."

The barman gives Charlie a sidelong glance.

"Ah, I get it," he says with a smile of complicity. "You want to talk to her... They'll all be coming here tonight to dance... But you have to be a member to get in. During the day you can come in here no problem, but at night it's impossible. I can tell by looking at you that you're no slouch with the ladies, but I'd be very surprised if that one would have anything to do with the son of a servant... But let me think for a bit... Not everyone here is a snob. I'll ask Hansy; his father's a rich industrialist, but he doesn't let that go to his head. That's it, I'll ask Hansy to invite you. So when you get here tonight, all you do is say you're a guest of Hansy and there won't be any problem..." He favours Charlie with a conspiratorial wink. "It's the least I can do for your father."

"Thank you, sir."

CHARLIE SITS in the sunlight watching the tennis match. Mademoiselle Abel is losing to a good-looking brunette. She's in a foul mood. Every time she misses a shot, Charlie applauds loudly. She looks quickly but furiously at the bleachers. At the end of the match (a terrific smash by her opponent that she could only watch as it went past her) Charlie jumps to his feet and claps. The two women pass in front of him. The winner (the brunette bombshell) smiles at him discreetly; Mademoiselle Abel looks straight ahead.

IN CHARLIE'S MINISCULE ROOM. Nine o'clock at night.
   "Who is it?"
   "Fanfan."
   "Come in."
   "What's happening, my man? You're all dressed up like a prince... You look like you got something big going on..."
   "How's your principal friend?"
   "I'm giving her a hard time... Chico says she drives past the Rex Café ten times an hour... You going to tell me where you're going?"
   "To the Bellevue Circle."
   "I hope you're a member, otherwise they'll kick your ass out of there...That place is like a fortress for the bourgeoisie, and they guard it very jealously, my friend...They'll card you..."
   "I got an invitation."
   "Oh, well, that's different..."
   "What's the matter, Fanfan? Why are you looking at me like that?"
   "If you want my advice, my friend, take off that suit, which you have obviously rented for the occasion."
   "But it's a good suit. You said yourself I look like a prince."

"Rule number one: don't dress like a prince when you're going among princes. You can't compete with them on their own ground."

"Okay, I understand... How do you know so much, anyway? You've never been invited into a rich person's home."

"I've prepared myself for that eventuality... And I'll give you some more advice, too: pretend to be honest. Don't try to hide anything. You're a poor man and they're rich, that's all. You could be introducing them to a whole new universe..."

"Look, Fanfan, I'm not going there to seduce the entire middle class. I'm going to meet a girl..."

"What I said goes for any and all occasions, my friend... See you around."

DOORMAN AT the entrance.

"You ain't a member."

"I'm a guest of Hansy's."

"Wait here."

He's gone for several minutes (I hope the barman didn't forget to warn Hansy), then comes back with a man who looks like a perpetual smiler, obviously a bon vivant.

"This guy says you invited him."

"Charlie! Charlie, my old buddy! What are you doing standing here at the door? Hey, Muscle," he says to the doorman, "don't you recognize Charlie? He won the German tennis championship, first Haitian to ever place in the top ten..."

Muscle gives Charlie a dubious look. He must be used to Hansy's shenanigans.

"Don't listen to him," Charlie says quickly. "I don't even know him. A friend of mine"—he didn't want to betray the barman—"asked him to invite me, seeing as I'm not a member."

This time the look Muscle gives him contains a degree of astonishment. Hansy laughs so hard his sides are aching.

"What a kidder," he says to Charlie, clapping him on the back.

Hansy shows Charlie around the club for a few moments. One of the morning's players, the brunette bombshell, comes up to them.

"Thanks for encouraging me this morning," she says with a slight American accent. She gives him a long, languorous wink.

"Don't mention it," Charlie says calmly, "I like the way you play..."

"Really? You have no idea how happy that makes me! Thank you so much." And she continues on her way, smiling.

"What did you say to her? I've never seen June so excited before... Did you see that wink she gave you?"

"She's a nice girl."

"What? A nice girl? She's marvellous, my friend. She's the most beautiful woman I know."

Hansy seems on the point of bursting with excitement.

"Don't mind me," he says, "I get like this... I'm hypersensitive, you see... But June... I've never seen her like this... And you take it so... casually... Oh, I see, she's not the right gender for you, is that it?"

Without Charlie being aware of it, someone has come up to stand beside Hansy.

One Good Deed

"Hansy, darling, what are you doing, talking to this imbecile?"

"Who do you mean, Missie?" Hansy says, looking frantically about.

"The idiot standing in front of you, Hansy."

"Him? Do you know him?"

"I saw him this morning."

"Ah!" says Hansy, laughing. "It was you playing June, was it? Florence called me to say June absolutely wiped the court with someone this morning, but she wouldn't tell me who it was..."

"Oh, stop it, Hansy. As for him, I don't know how he got in here, but..."

"He's here as my personal guest... a dear friend... Let me introduce you... In the left corner, Missie Abel, tolerable as a tennis player but intolerable off the court... And in the right corner, my good friend Charlie... Let the games begin..."

"I don't know where you dig up your dear friends, Hansy, but for heaven's sake you don't have to drag them in here..."

"I don't think I need to mention that no holds are barred."

"At any rate," Charlie says evenly, "I don't like bottle blondes. "

"What! Me, a bottle blonde! You're out of your mind! You don't know what you're talking about! You see, Hansy, I told you he was an idiot."

"And worse than bottle blondes," continues Charlie, "what I dislike even more are real blondes who never stop bragging about it."

Missie's mouth drops open.

"I'm going to get a whisky, Hansy," Charlie says. "Do you want a drink?"

"I'll have the same," Hansy replies. "What about you, Missie?"

"What?" says Missie.

"Do you want something? Charlie's getting the drinks."

"No," she says, barely managing a whisper.

Missie still seems to be suffering from shock.

"Technical knockout," Hansy says, ending the bout.

"DID YOU SEE Hansy?" asks the barman.

"Yes, sir."

"And how did it go with her?"

"The trap has been baited."

"Let me buy you a drink... What'll it be?"

"Two whiskies. I'll pay for Hansy's."

"Hey, now, you're not going to let yourself pay for these rich gents, are you? They're very good at that game... I'll give you two whiskies on the house. I'll put a little water in the bottle and keep it under the counter until the end of the evening, say around three in the morning, when all they'll taste is the fire... Don't worry, I've been here twenty years. I know the way things are around here. I served the fathers, and now I'm serving the sons."

Charlie goes back to Hansy, who is standing beside the battered old piano.

"No one but Jacky Duroseau can play this thing now. He completely wrecked it by pouring whisky all over it. When he drinks, he thinks the piano should drink, too. He's supposed to play every Saturday night, but he only shows up when he feels like it. Once he came on a Monday... You've brought me a drink. Thanks, Charlie."

"No problem... I didn't pay for it. The barman wouldn't take my money."

Hansy looks at him strangely.

"You always tell the truth, don't you? Around here everybody pretends... They even pretend to be rich, when in fact most of them are on the verge of bankruptcy... Don't you worry about old Samson, he'll top the bottle up with water. He thinks no one knows about it, but in fact everyone's figured out his little game. No one but ninnies buy drinks here after two AM... You see how they're looking at us? It's because they've heard about our little scene."

"What are you talking about?"

"Well, you just shut Missie's mouth for her. It appears she has locked herself in the john. I also told them about June. You know who June is, don't you? She's the daughter of the American consul. Not bad for a guy who isn't even a member of the Circle. As far as I'm concerned, you are a prince among men. Even Muscle is impressed, and no one impresses Muscle. He came up to me a while ago and asked me if it was true that you're a German tennis champion. Don't you realize what a stir you're creating? In one day you've made the inaccessible June lose her head and sent the acid-tongued Missie packing.

TEN MINUTES LATER.

"Missie is outside, Charlie. She wants to talk to you."

"No problem."

They go out.

"It's all your fault, Hansy," Missie says, just short of tears.

"What happened?"

"Everyone is saying I'm fighting with June over this... imbecile. You have a wicked, wicked tongue."

"Would you be good enough to tell me why you called me out here?" Charlie asks politely.

Missie turns on him.

"I want you to go back in there," she says breathlessly, "and tell everyone that I have absolutely no interest in you whatso-ever, and that I do not intend to fight over you with June."

"You'll have to run all that by me again, because I didn't understand any of it. And you talk too fast," Charlie adds with a half-smile.

She glares at him angrily.

"I could never feel anything for a person like you."

"What do you mean by that?" Hansy asks.

Charlie signals to him to stay out of it.

"But Hansy, I don't even know him. He isn't a member..."

"No, I am not a member of your charmed Circle. I know that. My mother is a governess and my father is a gardener... In other words, they're servants... They work not far from here..."

"And you dare to come in here?"

"Missie!" cries Hansy. "Don't you see how exceptional this fellow is? You're right, he's not at all like us. He has no desire to hide his origins, or his identity... There's not a single mem-ber of the Circle who hasn't been vague about his life from time to time. We're always lying about something, hiding our suffering, our desires, our fears... A man who can proclaim his agony like this fellow does is a prince, I tell you, a prince."

"Will you please leave us alone, Hansy?" Missie says.

Charlie and Missie watch Hansy move off towards the brightly lit building.

"Do you know why I'm here?"

"No, but I have a feeling you're going to tell me," Missie says, resuming her customary ironic tone ("acid-tongued Missie," as she is known).

"I happened to be in the area, and I saw you crossing the street, on your way to play tennis. And I said to myself, 'That's her. I want her. She's the one!' That's the only reason I came here tonight."

Missie looks at him, nearly choking.

"Me! You! Why?"

"That's the way it is. I want you... I want to hear you moan... and I will..."

Missie continues staring at him, transfixed.

"I'm in no hurry," Charlie says calmly.

And he leaves. Before Missie can even think of anything to say, he's at the gate of the Bellevue Circle. The meeting place of the privileged youth of Pétionville. Missie feels that she can no longer stop herself from retching. She bends over between two parked cars and vomits huge, yellow streams on the green grass.

She stays outside for a long time, watching the others dancing. She sees Hansy come out to look for her, but really, she doesn't feel up to talking to anyone. She runs between the luxurious cars parked anyhow on the lawn. She wants nothing more than to go home and shut herself up in her room. She hears Hansy calling, over and over. "That asshole has made me run away from my own friends twice in one night," she thinks, continuing to flee. A luminous white dress in the moonlight. Just before reaching the villa, she stops one more time to throw up.

TWO O'CLOCK in the afternoon. Someone knocks on the door to Charlie's miniscule room.

"Come in, it's open."

Hansy comes in.

"What did you do to Missie?"

"What are you talking about?"

"She's gone completely bonkers . . . She came to my place at nine o'clock this morning . . . Nine o'clock! I was barely awake! She wanted me to find you. We looked everywhere. I don't know what happened between the two of you, and it's really none of my business, but I think it must have been serious . . ."

"Where is she, Hansy?"

"She's downstairs in the car. I'll go tell her to come up, shall I? I'll stay down there."

Charlie dresses hurriedly. He starts tidying up the room, then changes his mind at the last moment. He decides to wait for Missie sitting on his narrow, iron bed.

She comes in.

One Good Deed

"Hello."

"Hello."

"Excuse me for bothering you at home like this, but I didn't sleep last night."

"Ah!"

"I don't understand what right you have to think of me that way," she says coldly.

"And that's why you came here, so I could explain it to you?"

A long moment of silence.

"It's because I'm afraid of voodoo."

He bursts out laughing.

"Is that it? Really?"

He laughs again, falling back on the bed.

"No," he says, "I don't use voodoo for things like this."

"What, then?"

"It's a question of blood."

"Blood?"

"Yes. My blood wants to mingle with your blood."

Missie's lips begin to tremble.

"I don't understand."

"What I mean is that it's out of control . . . It has nothing to do with religion, or race, or even sex."

"Well, if that's true, then it has nothing to do with me, either," she says, moving towards the door.

"If it had nothing to do with you, you wouldn't have come here."

She stops suddenly, like someone who has been shot in the back just as she was about to rush down the stairs.

CHARLIE IS LYING on his back, staring up at the ceiling. He can lie like this for hours.

"Can you lend me ten bucks, Charlie?" says Fanfan, coming into the room.

"Where do you think I could get hold of ten bucks?"

"Come on, Charlie, this is serious. I'm caught short. I'll pay you back first thing next week."

Charlie gets up and opens a drawer.

"Here. But you absolutely have to pay me back on Monday."

"Thanks, old pal, you've saved my life... By the way, how did things go last night at the Bellevue Circle?"

"As you suggested, I played the sincerity card, and so far it seems to have worked... I met that girl, Missie Abel..."

"Wait, I know that name... Isn't she the ambassador's daughter?"

"His niece."

"What happened?"

"She was here, just before you walked in."

"Ah, my friend, you're playing in the big leagues."

Fanfan pushes Charlie until he falls back on the bed.

"Listen, Fanfan, you haven't understood what I'm saying."

"You're going to tell me what it's like to pork a rich girl!"

Silence.

"No, Fanfan, she just dropped by to tell me that we're from two different worlds."

"In her eyes you're nothing but a dog."

"That's it."

Longer silence.

One Good Deed

"I've got to go, my friend ... Don't worry about your money. I'll have it here Monday without fail."

Fanfan misses a step on the stairway.

"Shit! Shit! Shit! And shit!"

TWO DAYS LATER. Two o'clock in the afternoon.

Charlie climbs heavily up the steep stairs to his room. Missie is waiting for him at the top.

"Have you been here long?"

She gives him a beseeching look.

"Did Hansy drop you off?"

"I took a taxi."

He opens the door and lets her go in first. She enters and sits on the only chair. Charlie remains standing. She sits there without saying a word. Then suddenly she jumps up.

"Goodbye."

She races down the stairs at the risk of breaking her neck. He listens for a moment, hoping she'll reach the bottom in one piece. Then he sits in the chair she has vacated, and waits.

He waits.

Two hours go by. She comes back. He hears her feathery tread on the stairs. He tells himself that her feet would do well to get used to climbing those stairs, because they're going to be climbing it many times a day from now on. A small knock at the door.

"It's open."

She comes in. He doesn't get up.

She stands in the middle of the room. He looks at her tranquilly.

"I can't do it anymore."

He keeps looking at her.

"I want..."

She stops, thunderstruck. A fierce storm appears to be raging in her head. He waits, silently.

"I want..."

She stops again.

"I want..."

Her knees buckle slightly.

"The other day you said, you said..."

"What did I say?"

A moment's hesitation. But she recovers. He has the feeling she may get away from him. Then she lowers her head.

"You said that you'll... make me... moan..."

Charlies says nothing.

"I don't know why," she goes on, "but since then I've been able to think of nothing else..."

He decides not to have her today. She is suffering, but her pain is her pleasure.

WEDNESDAY MORNING. As usual, he finds the gate open. His mother is peeling potatoes in the kitchen, which is clean and well lit. He sneaks up silently behind her back. She is singing "The Red Roses of Corfu." Her happiness song. The one she sings when she's happy.

"Oh, it's you," she says without turning around.

One Good Deed

"How are things?"

"Very good, my dear."

"And Papa?"

"Your father is very excited because he planted some birds of paradise; you know how difficult it is to get them to grow... Well, yesterday he called me out into the garden, where as you know I hate to go because of the anole lizards, to see their magnificent flowers. They really do look like birds. Even the Ambassador was impressed."

"And Mademoiselle Abel?"

His mother looks at him in astonishment.

"Why are you asking about her?"

"She and Papa weren't getting along, and, if I remember correctly, you were pretty worried about it."

"Oh, we hardly ever see her anymore. First she was always underfoot, now she doesn't even come home for dinner. And when she is here, she shuts herself up in her room."

"And that doesn't bother you?"

"No! Things are much better this way..."

"Okay, Mama, I've got to go."

"Already? Do you need money? I don't have much, but..."

"No, I'm fine."

"Are you sure you don't need anything?"

"I'm sure."

"Good. Don't forget to shut the gate behind you."

"Yes, Mama."

A Naïve Painting

I tell you it's springtime by placing
a couple in the centre of the landscape.
DAVERTIGE

MY NAME IS Laura Ingraham. I'm thirty-five years old. Men find me attractive because I am tall, slim and blonde, but they also find me a bit frightening because I'm a New York Jewish intellectual. I was born in New York, and have lived there all my life. I love that city. Especially its hardness. New York doesn't believe in tears, as does, say, Moscow. My favourite book is *Breakfast at Tiffany's*, by Truman Capote. I always keep it in my handbag and take it out whenever I have a spare minute somewhere. For a long time I worshipped Andy Warhol. I collected anything from that era (late sixties, early seventies), the time of The Factory, the Warhol studio. My biggest regret is that I was never at Studio 54 when Jackie Kennedy, Liza Minnelli and Bianca Jagger were there. My favourite type of man: Peter Beard, the photographer/adventurer. My favourite film: Woody Allen's *Manhattan*. I've seen it more than a dozen times. I also love men's underwear by Calvin Klein. Do you remember Diane Keaton wearing it in *Annie Hall*? Well, I wore the same kind for years, right up until the time one of my lovers (a music critic for *Rolling Stone*) told me that once you're past adolescence such things are ridiculous. But it wasn't ridiculous to me.

I HAVE ANOTHER side that no one knows about. My secret garden. It's a story that goes back to my childhood. I was five. One day my father brought home a small painting (a landscape) and hung it in my bedroom, above my bed. A simple landscape, of the naïve school. Sometimes, at night, when I was afraid, I would spend a long time looking at this painting (nature, benevolent, luminous), until eventually my nerves would settle down. Sometimes I would imagine living in my painting. Being born in such a place instead of in Manhattan. But I need both. My urban landscape and my imaginary one. Manhattan excites me. But the landscape calms me. I believe that this duality is part of my deepest nature. Like most excitable beings, I am capable of remaining calm and quiet for hours on end. My friends are totally unaware of this aspect of my personality. All they know is this woman who is capable of spending two hours in Bloomingdale's looking for a scarf to wear to a cocktail party that evening, then after the party running out to Queens to visit a some friends before ending the night at some trendy new club on Long Island. No matter what the hour, I never go home without stopping on Park Avenue to pick up some warm bagels. This is the girl, urban down to her fingernails, that my friends know (even my closest friends). However, I can also be this little country girl who gets up at the crack of dawn with the roosters and goes outside in bare feet to gather ripe fruit that has fallen to the ground overnight. Am I schizophrenic, like most of the people who live in this city? When I left my parents' house and rented a small apartment near Columbia University, the one thing I took with me was that little landscape painting. And the first thing I did was hang it in my bedroom. Whenever I happened to wake up in the middle of the night with a bad case of the sweats (loneliness, combined with fear), that painting (the sole constant in my life) was the only thing that would calm me down.

I STILL HAD no idea what country the painting came from. I could have found out easily enough, if I'd wanted to, by looking at a few art books in the Public Library, but I was never interested in the painting's origins. The landscape existed so concretely to me that I never thought of attaching it to any particular place. Except for the place that existed inside me. But I took that place with me wherever I went. One day I was meeting an old friend at a bar not far from MOMA (the Museum of Modern Art in New York), and as I was a bit early (a mania with me) I decided to kill some time at the museum. There happened to be an exhibition of Haitian naïve art. And there, to my astonishment, were these enormous canvases (enormous in their quality more than in their dimensions) in the same style as my little landscape. It wasn't so much that I had found a country; I had discovered a universe. An

A Naïve Painting

enchanted world. Brilliant colours. Animals, people (lots of people), mountains. Thatched huts on the flanks of blue mountains. Fish flying through the air. Cattle crossing swollen rivers. Cocks fighting. Marketplaces. Tall, slender women calmly walking down from the hills with heavy sacks on their heads. Children playing in dreamscapes. The sea. Everywhere, the sea. And no one looking at it. Natural life. Only after I had made a complete circuit of the exhibition did I begin to notice the names of the painters. The signatures danced in the corners of the canvases. Salnave Philippe-Auguste, the friend of the Douanier Rousseau ("I want to speak of Rousseau's *Dream*. Just as one could say that everything is contained in the *Apocalypse* of Saint John, so, I am tempted to say, this huge painting includes all poetry, and with it all the mysterious gestations of our time..."—André Breton, 1942). The quote was printed across the back wall of the room in which the massive jungle-scapes of Salnave Philippe-Auguste were hung. In another room: the imaginary villages of Préfète Duffaut. The maniacally delicate precision of Rigaud Benoît. Jasmin Joseph's candor. Saint-Brice, who drew me in and frightened me at the same time. And the immense Hector Hyppolite (a Homer who used colour instead of words). Most of all, what sealed my loyalty to these magical works was the natural way they dealt with death. Life and death intermingled. They even made me wonder if death didn't precede life. For me, who had always been afraid of the dark, this was the first time I had felt calm when confronted with symbols of death (especially in the paintings of André Pierre). I don't know what happened (the security guard came and cast an uneasy glance into the room, even though I was the only visitor), but I no longer felt as though a block of cement were sitting on my chest, preventing me from breathing, as I had felt since my childhood. These are my people! These are my people! These are my people! I must go back to my people! I felt like an animal that had strayed from its herd, and years later was beginning to find traces of it. I absolutely had to get myself down there immediately. It was a matter of life and death.

I LEFT NEW YORK the next day, and have been in Haiti ever since. I lived in Port-au-Prince for a few months (I couldn't stand the Bellevue Circle crowd for much longer, completely self-absorbed as they were; I wasn't interested in re-creating in Port-au-Prince the artificial life I had just left behind in Manhattan), and then I met Solé, a farmer from Artibonite, and followed him here. I look after the house and our son Choual (which means "Horse")—he's the little blond-haired black boy playing football down there with his schoolmates—and sell the produce from our rice fields. Artibonite is in the part of the country that produces the most rice. Our rice is very aromatic. It's the best in Haiti. If you're ever in the region of Haiti that includes Hinche, Verrettes, Petite Rivière, Pont Sondé, Marchand-Dessalines, Saint-Marc or even Gonaïves, ask for the white farmer, and they'll direct you to my house. My name is Laura Joseph. I'm now forty-seven years old, and I live with my husband and son in the painting of my childhood.

A Naïve Painting

A Small House on the Side of the Blue Mountain

THREE DAYS AGO, Rebecca, her husband and their three children (twin girls who are ten years old and a boy who is eight) arrived in Port-au-Prince. They're from London, where her husband runs an art gallery. Their friends call her Becky.

Becky is tall and blonde with a somewhat severe face. She has small breasts. Years ago she was a champion discus thrower.

Becky rides on the weekends on their large estate on the outskirts of London. Her family also owns vast lands in Australia and a huge house in the centre of the oldest part of London. Her father, a former officer in the Royal Navy, is also an accomplished athlete. Becky received a Spartan education. She wears jewelry only on rare occasions (a pearl necklace that her mother gave her as a wedding gift).

Everyone agrees that Becky is a good person. Stalwart, honest, old-fashioned. The typical British sporting type. She met her husband at a vernissage—she'd gone there with a woman friend—and they were married six months later. Rebecca Hunter has just turned forty, and this trip is, in some ways, a birthday present.

BECKY WANTED TO bring the children despite her mother's insistence that she keep them with her in London.

"Becky, don't you think John would like to have you to himself, without the children, just this once?"

"Don't argue, Mother. I'm bringing the children. They'll love the ocean. They'll have the mountains and the sea."

"Becky, perhaps I didn't make myself clear enough: there are times when a woman simply has to be a woman."

"What do you mean by that?"

Her mother looks her straight in the eye.

"Becky, you are forty years old, don't pretend you don't know what I'm talking about."

"Of course I do, Mother. It's just that I have no interest in being alone with John."

The older woman seems about to run her hands over a small African statue of a man with pronounced Negroid characteristics, but changes her mind at the last minute. Her hand remains open but still, a sign of her own nervousness.

"You don't love your husband?"

"That's not the point, Mother."

"He neglects you."

"Mother, when are you going to understand that such things don't interest me in the least?"

The mother takes several quick steps about the room before turning again to her daughter.

"You prefer women?"

"What are you talking about, Mother!"

"I know what I'm talking about. You can be frank with me."

"No, Mother! I am not even remotely interested in women."

A Small House on the Side of the Blue Mountain

"Well, then, in whom *are* you interested?"

"I keep busy with the children, with the horses, with visiting my friends in the country. That's what I like doing."

"And your husband?"

"My husband is my husband."

"I'm going to tell you this for the last time, Becky: we women are much more complicated than you seem to think. In any case, you'll see for yourself..."

Becky looks at her for a moment. They are standing at the centre of the great hall in the Hunter house in London, surrounded by life-sized African statues, huge elephant tusks, some quite frightening Beninese masks, hunting trophies and magnificent warrior lances belonging to Colonel Hunter's famous collection.

"Well, I must run, Mother. I still haven't bought the children's bathing suits..."

"Bon voyage, my dear."

"It's only for eight days, Mother. You'll see the kids again soon enough. I promise I'll take good care of them."

THE CHILDREN DIDN'T sleep for the entire flight. They were disagreeable the whole time, and Becky had to get cross with them several times. John-John wanted to go to the toilet no fewer than eight times, his revenge for having to sit still, which he hates more than he hates broccoli. Each time, Becky had to go with him. As for John, he sat reading *The Economist* throughout the whole flight. The twins never stopped bickering. By the time the airplane touched down in Port-au-Prince, Becky was exhausted. A bus was waiting to take them (and

several other of the passengers) out of the capital, to a pictur-
esque little village they had chosen from a tourist brochure.

"Look, Mother," cries John-John. "The houses all look like
they're made for children."

"No," John mutters. "They're made for tourists."

"Would you please keep your cynicism to yourself, John,"
Becky all but snaps at him.

"Look!" cry the twins in chorus. "The sea!"

The bus has taken a road that cuts through dark-brown
land above a turquoise sea. On the opposite side of the road,
a field of sugar cane stretches to the horizon. A light breeze
teases dust into the air, preventing the driver from going too
fast. They pass a black-clad woman walking behind a donkey.

"Look!" cries one of the twins. "A donkey!"

In the distance they can see the blue mountain. With a
small house on the side.

"I could easily live here," Becky sighs, "in that little shack."

Her husband gives the house a brief glance.

"Not me," he says dryly.

"I wasn't thinking of you," she murmurs, as though speaking to herself.

Another moment and the bus pulls up in front of a small
hotel sitting lopsidedly beside the road.

"It looks like a primitive painting," says one of the twins.

THEY UNPACK QUICKLY. The children have a light snack,
and then everyone lies down for a nap. Except Becky. Oddly
enough she no longer feels exhausted, despite the extraor-
dinarily lengthy and trying trip. After long deliberation she

A Small House on the Side of the Blue Mountain

chooses a yellow dress and a pair of white pumps in which to go exploring. The hot air hits her square in the face, but she feels fine, so far from London. The more she walks, the less tired she becomes. Suddenly she feels she could walk like this without ever stopping or retracing her steps. At a crossroads she comes upon a man who appears to be having trouble with his horse.

"May I help you?"

The man turns quickly and looks at her, this stranger, before going back to struggling with the animal.

"Let me do it," she says in a voice that commands authority.

She takes the horse by its head and, stroking it, removes the bit that has become wedged in its mouth. It takes her at most ten seconds. The man thanks her curtly, removing his hat, then turns and lets the horse run off towards the mountain.

Becky returns to the hotel. The red sun is already half-submersed in the sea.

THE NEXT MORNING, Becky wakes before the others and goes downstairs to take her coffee before the dining room fills up. An enormous woman with a perpetually smiling face is waiting for her.

"Madame Hunter?"

"Yes."

"Somebody left this package for you last night."

"But I don't know anyone here."

"A man who says you helped him with his horse."

"So I did. He didn't seem too happy about it."

"He's always like that."

"Ah," says Becky, her interest aroused, "you know this man?"

"I've seen him around. I don't know his name. He never speaks to anyone. They say he comes from a village in the northern part of the country. They're a proud people up there."

"What's he doing down here?" Becky asks, a little sharply.

"I don't know... Nobody knows... Look, madame, you can see his little shack from here..."

"Which one?"

"That one... he built it himself, barely a month ago. Around here, when a man builds a house, it's usually for a woman."

"Oh?"

"But he doesn't have a woman," the innkeeper adds, wearily.

Becky opens the package.

"Oh!" exclaims the innkeeper. "Those are scented herbs."

She takes a handful of the herbs and presses them to her nose.

"Smell them," she says. "They smell awfully good."

Becky finds herself suddenly inundated with the aroma of the Caribbean.

"Whatever am I going to do with them?" she says, her voice at once delighted and astonished.

"Put them everywhere about yourself, madame... In your bath, in your room, on your bed, on your clothes."

"But why did he give me this gift?"

The fat innkeeper bursts out laughing. Her whole body shakes.

"Here, when a man gives you scented herbs, it means he wants you..."

A Small House on the Side of the Blue Mountain

"Wants me for what?" Becky asks, panicking slightly.

"He wants you, madame."

She continues laughing. Becky gets up from the table a bit shakily, like an inexperienced boxer who's been rabbit-punched just as she turned to the referee.

THE LITTLE TRIBE spent the day at the beach. They sang all the way back to the hotel.

"What the devil does he want, I wonder?" John mutters sullenly.

"Who?" asks Becky.

"Him, he's been following us. He seems to want to talk to you."

"Maybe he wants something..."

"He doesn't look like a beggar or whatever they call them down here," John says. "And I don't like the way he smiles," he adds.

"I don't know him," Becky says, almost casually.

"I'm going to ask him what he wants."

"Oh, leave him be, John."

"What he wants," she thinks, and the thought frightens her, "is your wife."

AS SOON AS they enter their room, Becky calls out:

"Everyone in the shower, and be sure to wash your hair thoroughly."

"Yes, Mommy," says one of the twins. "Salt water is bad for your hair."

"You've told us often enough," says the other one.

"I don't like you being so sassy," Becky says in mock anger. "John-John, try not to get sand everywhere."

"But Mommy..."

"No 'but Mommy,' please. I have a terrible headache..."

"Come on, Becky," says John. "Relax. We're on vacation."

"Easy for you to say," Becky spits at him. "With your nose stuck in a magazine all day."

The children decamp to the bathroom.

"What's got into you?"

"Nothing. It's just seeing your face. It depresses me."

"Why? What have I done?"

"Nothing... I'm just having one of my migraines."

"Is it your period, dear?"

"Damn it, John!"

THE CHILDREN APPEAR to have finished their showers.

"I want you to tidy up the bathroom... I don't want to find hair all over the place, do you hear me?"

"Yes, Mommy," in chorus.

"Dry your hair thoroughly, and when you're finished you can run me a bath."

"If it's all right with you," John says, "I'd like to take a shower first."

John heads for the bathroom. Becky stares at her shaking hands. "Good Lord," she thinks. "What's come over me?"

"Bring me a comb and a brush and I'll do your hair now... John-John, dry yourself properly, you're not a baby anymore..."

A Small House on the Side of the Blue Mountain

John-John's sad look. Three days ago Becky would have taken him in her arms and consoled him. Now she is unmoved. And John-John senses the change: he dries himself methodically without taking his eyes off his mother.

"That enough. Go get dressed now. And no squabbling, you three!"

John's voice from the bathroom. And the sound of his electric razor.

"Would you like me to run your bath, my dear?"

Becky decides not to answer him.

"I asked if you still want to take a bath."

Silence.

"Have you changed your mind, or do you still want a bath?"

"Damn it, John!"

"Can I not even talk to you anymore?"

"I have had it up to here with your stupid questions!"

"I've never seen you behave this way before. Are you nervous about something?"

Becky tightens her grip on the comb and brush to stop her hands from trembling. She exhales through her mouth, a thin stream of air.

"Are you pregnant?"

"By whom would I be?"

"What a question!" John exclaims, laughing.

An embarrassed laugh.

THREE SMALL RAPS on the bathroom door.

"Who is it?" she says dryly.

"It's me, Mommy," comes John-John's small, frightened voice.

"Come in, sweetie."

John-John opens the door and remains in the doorway, his eyes filled with tears.

"What is it, John-John?"

"You don't love me anymore."

Becky isn't prepared for this stab in the back.

"Why do you say that? It's just that Mommy's tired."

John-John's sad, closed expression.

"You don't love us anymore."

"But what makes you say such a thing?"

"You're not here... You're not with us..."

"But look, here I am, sweetie! How can you say such a thing? Whatever do you mean?"

John-John remains silent, having nothing to add. He has said everything. Now there is only his limitless sadness.

"Come here, my sweet, come and give Mommy a hug... There, can you feel Mommy's here now?"

John-John smiles.

"It smells good in here, Mommy."

"It's these scented herbs, my little sweetie-pie."

"Am I still your sweetie-pie?"

"Of course you are, my darling..."

AT LAST BECKY is alone. She thinks about what her mother told her about the fact of being a woman. A woman alone with a man. With a man who wants her. She also thinks about the little house on the side of the blue mountain.

A Small House on the Side of the Blue Mountain

She feels like a traveller who, after an absence of many years, has finally come home. Having seen all the wonders of the world, the only thing that still has the power to move her is her little house.

Becky finds herself wondering if perhaps nature has nothing to do with things that happen on the surface. Things like colour, race, nationality, class, social structure. It does what it does. Deep below appearances. Unconcerned with surfaces.

She feels that everything is pulling her away from John, pulling her towards this man whose name she doesn't even know. Could this be possible?

Maybe people's names are also meaningless? Nature is deaf, dumb and blind. Then why did it put me in London and give me blonde hair and green eyes, if, in reality, I'm nothing but a simple peasant from the south of Haiti?

Nature makes no reply to that question, either.

JOHN SENSES THAT Becky is no longer beside him in bed. Without opening his eyes he runs his hand over her cold pillow. "She's probably in the bathroom," he thinks. When they were first married she would often spend a large part of the night sitting on the toilet seat, holding her head in her hands. When he would ask her what she was doing she would invariably reply that she couldn't breathe lying next to him.

"My darling, do you not feel well?"

No response.

"Shall I fetch a doctor?" he would ask, wondering where on earth he would find a decent doctor at that godforsaken hour of night.

Now he asks himself why on earth they are not taking their vacation in Rome, or Madrid, or New York, or even Kingston. Becky is right, when it comes down to it: he doesn't involve himself enough in such matters. He goes along with things too mechanically. Just now, for example, he's asking the same questions and pulling the same answers out of the same old bag of tricks he's been using for more than twenty years. He really thinks he's lost his taste for risk.

Moments later he is still wondering if he should get up or go back to sleep. He decides to get up.

"Becky! What are you doing?"

The children are sleeping on the floor in their blue sleeping bags. John remembers buying them on a rainy day in London. John-John looks like a little pageboy he saw a few years ago in the Prado. He glances tenderly at the two girls. They look like Siamese twins, curled up together like that in one sleeping bag. He goes downstairs, telling himself there is no need to hurry. The fat innkeeper is already calmly sipping a cup of coffee.

"Would you like a cup, monsieur?"

The smell of coffee and the weak morning light fill the tiny room with a degree of intimacy.

"I'm looking for my wife."

"Hmm."

"Do you know where she is?"

"Yes," the fat woman replies tranquilly. "She asked me to tell you."

"Ah! I should have guessed. She's gone for a walk on the beach," he says, feeling some colour come back to his cheeks.

A Small House on the Side of the Blue Mountain

"No, she went off towards the mountain . . ."

"Do you know which side?"

"Yes," says the fat woman in a neutral tone that he finds almost alarming.

"You have the advantage of me, madame," John says, in his British tone of voice.

He is no longer a frightened man; he is now an Englishman talking to an inferior.

"Come over here, monsieur," says the innkeeper with a tiny smile on her lips, a smile that is all but invisible to the naked eye . . . "Do you see that little house up there?"

"Yes."

"That's where you will find your wife."

John blanches.

"What's she doing up there?" he cries out, then immediately regains control of himself.

"When you go up the road, turn right and take the first path you see on your left . . . Are you with me, monsieur?"

"Yes," he says, his voice level.

"Take the first path you come to on your left . . . It will take you right up to the little house . . . You can't miss it."

"Thank you."

"Don't worry about the children," she says, her voice filled with kindness. "I'll look after them."

"How much do I owe you?"

"Nothing, monsieur," she says, laughing discreetly. "I advise you to get going before the sun gets too hot . . . You don't have your hat?"

"Yes, I have a hat... But I left it back there..."

"I'll go get it for you."

"I mean I left it in London."

"I see... Here, take this one, otherwise the sun will cook you like a crayfish... It's a good hour's walk for someone like you, who isn't used to climbing."

"What's the way again?"

"I told you, monsieur, take the road that runs past the hotel here, then turn left and keep to your right... There's nothing to it..."

THE SUN'S EFFECTS quickly make themselves felt. John sets himself a swift pace. His eyes are glued to the little house. "It's true, it's a nice house!" he tells himself. "But what is Becky doing in it? Maybe she wants to buy the place, keep it for a vacation home. Is she planning it as a surprise for me?" He has to admit he has no idea what Becky could be thinking. "She's English, like me. We have both always lived in London. We've been sleeping in the same bed for going on fifteen years. We have had three magnificent children together. I call her 'my sweet.' She calls me 'John.' Funny that she's never called me anything else. Diana"—his mistress—"calls me 'my little toad.' It's stupid, but at least she makes an effort. That's the thing, Becky never makes the least effort to create any kind of intimacy between us. At times I even get the feeling we've never made love together. The only things that really interest her are her horses. That perfectly composed expression at the height of our lovemaking (our monthly lovemaking), devoid

A Small House on the Side of the Blue Mountain

of emotion, like the flame of a candle during a momentary lull in the wind. That's the only Becky I've ever known in bed. It's true that she takes perfectly good care of the children. But what the devil is she doing in that little house, which seems to get farther away the faster I approach it?"

SHE IS STANDING on the balcony, leaning lightly against its centre-post.

"What are you doing here?" John asks.

"Poor you, you're completely covered in sweat! Come and sit down, I'll fetch you a glass of water."

She disappears into the house and returns almost immediately with a glass of ice-cold water.

"But what are you doing here, Becky?"

"You're repeating yourself, John. I heard you the first time."

"But you haven't answered me."

"Catch your breath... That final slope is quite steep."

"I don't understand, Becky."

"He built this house for me," she says, using a voice he has never heard from her before.

"Whom are you talking about?"

"Do you remember, John, as soon as I saw this house I felt something like a punch in my solar plexus?"

"You want to buy it, is that it?"

"From this moment on, John, this is where I live."

"Oh, right, I get it... We're going to spend the rest of our time here, just so that you..."

"You are deliberately misunderstanding me... I have a man in my life now, and this is where he lives."

"Have you lost your mind?"

"Absolutely not."

"What about the children?"

"Mother will help out with them... She's always dreamed of keeping them with her."

"You would leave the children, Becky?"

"Don't make this difficult, John, you won't get me back with such talk... I've done the math. I'm forty years old. In ten years, I'll be fifty, and it'll be too late for me. Whereas you, you'll just be starting to chase after girls fresh out of school."

"I won't leave you, Becky."

"Look, John, I have fifteen good years left in me, and I have no intention of spending them either with you or in London."

"But the children? Do you think I'm going to look after them for you?"

"Put them in an orphanage, John. You pay enough in taxes, surely the government will allow you that privilege..."

And she laughs. A laugh he has not heard before, either. Does he know her at all?

"Who is it? Someone who was in the plane with us, I'll wager."

"You've taken your time, John... I expected that to be your first question."

"Don't be sarcastic, Becky. It doesn't suit you."

"Ah, so suddenly you're an authority on what suits me... You've seen him, yesterday afternoon..."

A Small House on the Side of the Blue Mountain

"I didn't see anyone yesterday afternoon."

"Good heavens, John, you not only saw him, you pointed him out to me. You said he'd been following us for some time."

"But that was just some peasant I saw..."

"You are sitting in his house."

"I don't understand. Whose house?"

"My man's house."

"What are you saying? That peasant is your man? Since when?"

"Since last night. Don't force me to supply you with details, John. In any case, here he comes..."

"Where?"

"Turn around, you'll see him."

The man is climbing the final steep approach to the house. He moves with a certain agility. As he comes up he removes his jacket and greets John with a smile that is both timid and proud. The farmers in northern Haiti are known for their extreme politeness. John shakes his hand. Becky smiles.

Harry at Large

FOR ONCE, CHARLIE is on time. Fanfan has been waiting for him in the Rex Café, reading a Carter Brown.

"Sorry, old chum," Charlie says when he arrives. "But the damn streets are impossible this morning. There's a traffic jam stretching from the Au Beurre Chaud bakery all the way down to Firestone."

"That's not the way you come..."

"I'm telling you what it's like out there. Don't you listen to the radio?"

"Never. In any case, you're not late."

"What do you mean?"

"It's eleven o'clock. I told you to be here at nine just to make sure you'd be here at eleven."

"But it's not even eleven yet, Fanfan..."

"Exactly... It's five to eleven. So you see, you're on time."

Charlie sits down and signals the waiter to bring him his usual (a sandwich and a glass of papaya juice).

"I can't believe you would do that to me..." he says. "I cancelled quite a few meetings to be here..."

"I don't know what you're going on about... We were supposed to meet here at eleven, and you got here at five to. What time were you planning to get here?"

Charlie shakes his head sadly.

"You've just screwed up my entire schedule."

"Since when have you had a schedule?"

"It's all written down in here," he says, pointing his index finger to his temple.

The waiter arrives with a cup of steaming coffee and sets it down in front of Fanfan, who takes three large sips from it at the risk of burning his tongue.

"What are we doing now?" Charlie asks.

"We're waiting... That's what happens when you arrive someplace early."

"Oh, for Christ's sake..."

Fanfan laughs quietly.

"What does this guy want, anyway?"

"What do you think he wants?"

"Sex?"

"Are you gassed up?"

"Good, when is he supposed to get here?"

"Don't worry, he's an American... He'll be on time. Here he is now!"

The man walks into the narrow café and heads straight towards the only two customers sitting at a table. He sits down without introducing himself.

"A friend told me about you."

"About who?"

"Which one of you is Fanfan?"

"Bingo! I win! Am I allowed to know who my publicist is?"

"A woman you've been seeing."

"So what do you want," Charlie asks dryly.

"I gather you know a lot of girls..."

"What makes you think that?"

"I've been watching you since..."

The waiter comes over with a plate that he sets down in front of Charlie.

"Man, I'm starved."

Harry watches him literally gulp his sandwich and wash it down with long swallows of papaya juice.

"I've bought a small house down by the sea," Harry finally says, "and I want to invite a few friends over."

"Well, what do you know!" Fanfan says sarcastically. "Who'd have thought you'd come all the way down here to invite us to your little beach party?"

"No," Harry says deliberately. "I only want girls."

"So?" Charlie yelps.

"So, if you agree to lend us some of your little friends..."

"I don't get it," Charlie says.

"What don't you get, Charlie? This gentleman wants us to lend him some girls for his friends. That's not so hard to understand, is it? Sometimes you lend me your motorbike, don't you..."

"That's not the same thing!"

"Well, we're not talking about a motorbike, that's true. We're talking about that big, black car outside, which I suppose is his."

"So what do we get in return?"

Harry at Large

"I don't know, Charlie. Why don't you ask the man yourself..."

"Right... So what do we get in return?"

A long silence.

"You're not about to tell me that you have a little present for us, I hope?" says Charlie.

"You might take that as an insult."

"Yes, an insult," Charlie nods. "We might feel deeply offended..."

"Listen," says Harry. "I could see that you both get an American visa."

"And how are you going to do that?"

Harry smiles thinly.

"Don't you worry about that. I have some friends who could look after it..."

"Hey, I don't even know who you are," says Charlie. "Getting an American visa isn't easy."

"Don't mistake us for a couple of imbeciles," Fanfan adds.

Harry gives his characteristic laugh once more.

"There won't be any problem..."

"Okay," says Fanfan, "we believe you... Give us the visas, and we'll get you the girls.. ."

"Now who's taking who for an imbecile?" Harry slips in.

They all laugh this time.

"Good, okay then..." says Fanfan.

"Can I ask you a question?" Charlie says.

"Shoot."

"With your loot you could buy all the girls you want... Why do you want us to find them for you?"

"I'm not interested in whores! I'm asking only for normal girls... girls who come from normal families, neither rich nor poor... Normal girls."

"What do you mean, normal girls?"

"Your sister, for example! He wants you to bring him your sister, Fanfan."

Harry's face clouds over.

"No, no, nothing like that..." he says quickly.

"I was just joking," Charlie says. They know what Harry wants.

All the same, Harry finds himself on slippery ground.

"Okay, I've got to go... I'll let you know as soon as I've organized one of my little parties..."

"What about our visas?" Fanfan asks.

"You'll get them after there've been a few parties..."

"How many parties?"

"Let's just say when everyone's satisfied," Harry says in parting, heading for the door.

"DOES THAT IDIOT think we fell for his story?" Fanfan says after a while.

"I think he's serious..."

"Why do you think that?"

"He works at the American Embassy."

"Ah, does he?"

"I've seen him before, at the Bellevue Circle," Charlie says. "He's the father of one of the tennis players. A good-looking girl, June..."

Harry at Large

"Something about him gives me the creeps… That laugh…"

"Who set up this meeting?"

"Denz."

"Denz!" Charlie exclaims.

"He told me there was some guy who wanted to talk to us…"

"Did you know he was an American?"

"No, all I knew was that he was white."

"So what do you think?"

"Nothing," says Fanfan, shrugging his shoulders.

A Country Wedding

I'D COMPLETELY FORGOTTEN about the exhibition, the latest paintings of the artist Jacques Gabriel that are being shown in this tiny gallery in Pétionville. Even though my friend Carl-Henri has been going on and on about Gabriel for some time. Jacques this and Jacques that. To him, Jacques Gabriel is a kind of demigod: talented, modern, iconoclastic, liberated. He's also possessed of a pair of finely tuned antennae when it comes to picking up the tiniest political nuances, a trait that served him well (living dangerously on the edge as he does) during the strange universe of the Duvalier years. He maintains a complex network of friends, scattered here and there around the world, who keep him in touch with the latest movements in art (although he remains faithful to the frigid surrealism of Max Ernst). And he seems able to cross the barriers of social class with ease. He is equally at home with the wife of the French ambassador as with the young prostitute he picked up in the Macaya Bar, and who goes everywhere with him. He treats the prostitute as though she were a grand lady, and the ambassador's wife as though she were a prostitute. And both of them seem delighted by the novelty of it.

When I get there the reception (at least the official party) is over, but a few people (a restrained group of the artist's personal friends and admirers) are hanging around on the sidewalk, in front of the gallery.

Carl-Henri welcomes me with a conspiratorial smile, and introduces me to Jacques Gabriel. Tall, shaved head, insolent mouth, a man who intimidates from the word go. But the next second he favours me with a warm look that makes me reconsider my first impression.

"The vernissage is over," he says, brusquely enough.

"I didn't come to see the paintings..."

Carl-Henri turns pale.

"No?" says Gabriel, taken aback.

"I suppose I'm a bit old-fashioned..."

"Meaning what?" Gabriel tosses back, his tone hard.

"Well, meaning I like to meet the man before I get to know his work."

Gabriel looks at me in astonishment, then smiles.

"Me too! I'm the same way... If I don't like the man, I'm not interested in his work no matter how brilliant it is... It's a pleasure to meet a young man who knows how to think for himself..."

"Now you sound like a old asshole..."

Carl-Henri turns a shade paler. I feel sorry for his poor heart.

"Jacques," puts in one of the women, "it looks as though you've met your match..."

"Shut your face!" Gabriel bays at her. "And stop thinking with your vagina... You couldn't care less whether he's my match or not... All you want to know is whether you can take him home with you tonight..."

"Oh! Jacques!" she says in her pretty, pouting voice.

Everyone laughs (even the woman who's been attacked). The iconoclastic painter Jacques Gabriel has just used the old, tried and true trick of insulting a member of the bourgeoisie in order to bring the rest of the crowd over to his side.

"He's not always like this," Carl-Henri whispers.

"We're going to Croix-des-Bouquets, do you want to come?" Gabriel asks me, almost defiantly, or at any rate in a tone of voice different from the one he uses to address the others, even Carl-Henri.

"I'll come."

A generous burst of laughter from the painter.

"Good, let's go! Everyone to the cars. Carl-Henri, you," (he nods to me with an irresistible smile) "Fifi," (the little prostitute) "M.R." (a Parisian journalist who is doing a profile of Gabriel for her magazine) "... you all come in my car. The rest of you can make your own way there," he adds, laughing.

Jacques Gabriel drives without the slightest regard for the rules of the road. Fortunately, we get through Port-au-Prince without incident, unless you count the daggers drawn between the journalist (very pretty, but a total snob) and the painter! The second car falls farther and farther behind.

"What do you think about power?" she asks him point blank.

"I'm not interested in generalities," Gabriel replies.

"I'm talking about the way you yourself use power."

Brief silence.

"Would you care to be more specific, madame?"

A Country Wedding

"Sure," she says, taking a deep breath. "Just a few minutes ago, with that young woman."

"What did I do to her?"

The journalist looks somewhat astonished at the painter's disingenuousness.

"You insulted her."

"I simply told her the truth . . . It's what I thought she was thinking."

"Ah, so you really believe women think about nothing but that?"

The car swerves sharply towards the side of the road.

"Never use generalities when you're speaking to me. That's the last time I'm going to tell you!"

The darkness is total. We're driving through a complete blackout. Every now and then we pass a truck with a load of passengers. Jacques Gabriel's game seems fairly simple: he heads straight for the truck as it comes towards us, forcing it to move over to make room for us to pass. At first I thought he didn't know how to drive, or that he was drunk, but now I realize he knows full well what he's doing. It's a trick invented by truck drivers a long time ago, and Gabriel is simply giving them a taste of their own medicine. We've completely lost sight of the second car.

"What about you, how do you use power?" Gabriel says roughly.

"Who?" says the journalist, surprised.

"You."

"I don't know what you're talking about," she says tautly.

"I was watching you earlier at the gallery."

"But I didn't do anything! What did you see?"

"Exactly!" Gabriel shouts, and gives a brief burst of a laugh. "You did nothing!"

"So?" asks the journalist, still tense.

"You know very well, my dear, that you don't need to do anything. That servile bunch of bourgeois in Pétionville are ready to throw themselves at your feet... Those know-nothings would sell their first-born to be talked about in Paris. To them, talking to a special emissary from a big magazine is like talking to Paris itself... But I can assure you, madame, that the rest of the country is quite different... We're neither French living in America nor Africans living in exile. We're Haitians, know what I'm saying?... No, there's no way you could understand. Maybe you'll catch on eventually..."

Just as the journalist leans forward with fire in her eyes to say something in reply to Gabriel's accusation of colonialism (the worst thing a Parisian leftist journalist can be accused of), the car runs over something with a dull thud.

"Oh! *Vierge Marie!*" cries the little prostitute.

"It must have been a wild goat or something crossing the road," says Carl-Henri.

Jacques Gabriel pulls the car over. When he gets out, he finds that he has indeed hit a wild goat. There is the odour of hot blood. But rather than get back in the car, Gabriel walks off into the canefield with the dead animal in his arms.

"What's he doing?" gasps the journalist.

"*Lal fé poul sa'l gin poul fé,*" says the little prostitute.

The journalist looks at Carl-Henri.

"What did she say?"

A Country Wedding

"She said that Jacques Gabriel is doing what he has to do."

The journalist makes a scornful face.

"You don't believe in invisible forces?" I ask her.

"Sorry," she says with a smile. "I'm not the least bit superstitious."

"It's not necessarily superstition," says Carl-Henri.

"As far as I'm concerned," she says, "this car has run over a wild goat."

"*Cé sa ou pensé*," says the little prostitute, who understands a bit of French but doesn't speak it.

The journalist jumps as though her body has received an electric shock. Without knowng exactly what the prosititute has been saying in Creole, she is convinced that the woman has been speaking to her and that her words are filled with venom. She suspects that Carl-Henri has been discreet in his translations. On the surface of it, the little prostitute hasn't said anything particularly vindictive. She simply said: "That's what you think." Nonetheless, the journalist has good reason to be suspicious: it's a safe bet that if they were in a dark alley somewhere in Port-au-Prince the little prostitute wouldn't hesitate for a second to slit her throat. Why? Because, daughter of the Gonaïves that she is, she has always known who her enemies are. To test this theory, M.R. (the woman, not the journalist) turns to the little prostitute, who is sitting behind her, but cannot bring herself to stare into the flame of pure hatred that burns in her eyes.

And then Jacques Gabriel comes out of the canefield with the goat across his shoulders. With a shrug he drops the animal into the trunk at the back of the car.

"What a strange man," the journalist says. "A moment ago he was carrying the goat in his arms as though the car had run over a child, not an animal, and now here he is just dumping it into the trunk."

"Now," says Carl-Henri, "it's just so much meat..."

"What happened between then and now?" asks the journalist, intrigued.

"Ah, that you'll have to ask Jacques."

Jacques Gabriel settles himself behind the wheel. The journalist wisely decides not to question him about the goat. We drive for ten or fifteen minutes before turning left onto a red-ochre road that climbs fairly steeply up a slope and ends at a small shack with a thatched roof.

"Everyone out," says Jacques Gabriel. "This is where my friend the Prophet lives... Wait here, I'll go in first."

We wait for ten or fifteen minutes and then Gabriel comes out accompanied by a tall man with a grave expression on his face.

"This is my friend the Prophet. He's a great painter... Blessed by the gods of voodoo... He dwells in the depths where gods speak directly to men..."

The Prophet smiles. A smile of infinite sadness.

"I knew you were coming," he says simply, then turns and goes back towards his house.

Jacques Gabriel gets the goat and gives it to a young man who has appeared suddenly among us. The young man takes it and vanishes as swiftly as he appeared.

"The Prophet's working," says Jacques Gabriel. "He's making a painting to celebrate our arrival. He'll join us later."

A Country Wedding

The young man comes back with a few straw chairs that he arranges in a semicircle on the verandah. While he's at it, I see an enormous woman passing, accompanied by a dozen young girls in white robes with their heads wrapped in white kerchiefs.

"The Prophet is first and foremost a voodoo priest," Jacques Gabriel explains. "He started painting by making an altar to attract the gods. One day a man named DeWitt Peters, an American who was into Haitian painting, came by, and spent the whole day looking at the portraits of voodoo gods that the Prophet had painted on the walls of his house, and in the end came to the conclusion that the Prophet was the most authentic artist he had ever encountered."

"How does that differentiate him from you?" asks the journalist, who has just remembered she has to write an article about Jacques Gabriel.

Gabriel drags a chair closer to the door and sits down. This is going to take a while.

"The Prophet isn't his real name... He's been called that since he was nine years old. He was living in Dondon, a commune near Saint-Raphaël, with his mother and his younger sister. His father had left to cut cane in the Dominican Republic. At that time he still hadn't learned to talk. He couldn't read or write. When he wanted to tell someone something, he drew it."

"Interesting," says the journalist, "but not particularly unique."

"He has another gift. He can draw the future."

"How's that again?" I ask.

Jacques Gabriel smiles. The fish has taken his bait.

"One day he comes home from school. His mother is making dinner. He refuses to touch the food. He takes out his pocketknife and draws a headless man lying on a large mahogany table. His mother is amazed. 'It's my father,' he says simply. An hour later a messenger arrives with the news that his father is dead. 'How did he die?' the mother asks. She's told that there was a violent argument with another worker in a canefield at San Pedro de Macorís, and that the other man cut off the father's head with a single swipe of his machete. A week later, the boy draws a house in flames. That same night a fire completely destroys the house next door. Another time he draws his cousin with a single leg. The cousin lived in Saint-Raphaël. The next day his leg gets caught in a piece of mill machinery and has to be cut off to prevent the rest of the body from being pulled in. The mother refuses to allow the boy to do any more drawings. Then one morning, before going to the Ranquitte market to sell her vegetables, the mother says to him, 'Why don't you draw any more pictures?' To which the boy replies, 'But Mama, you told me I couldn't!' 'Ah, yes, I forgot! Make me a drawing now.' So the boy goes into the house and makes the drawing. When he comes back out, she has already left for the market. The drawing shows a woman lying in a coffin. After her death, the villagers in Dondon start calling him the Prophet. He's travelled pretty much all over the country, but eventually settled here in Croix-des-Bouquets. He serves his gods, lives with these women, indifferent to fame. His art is celebrated the world over. So that's the Prophet, the only completely free man I know."

A Country Wedding

"Why is that?" Carl-Henri asks, almost timidly.

"Well! Every time he takes up a paintbrush he knows that he might be about to paint his own death scene, and yet his hand never trembles."

The young man comes out with a large bowl balanced on his head. Behind him come the girls, in single file, with the large woman bringing up the rear. He sets the bowl down among us. It is filled with food—goat stew, peeled bananas, white rice, yams, breadfruit, carrots, beets, eggplant and cream sauce.

"No utensils!" Jacques Gabriel cries delightedly. "We eat with our fingers, our good old fingers..."

Brief silence.

"Won't it be too hot?" asks the journalist.

"It'll be fine!" says Gabriel, plunging his hand into the middle of the bowl.

That's the signal. We are all, it seems, famished.

I don't know if it's all these happenings, or the strange atmosphere (the starless night, the light breeze, the distant beating of a drum), the tender flesh of the goat (was it an animal or something else entirely?), or the subtle aroma of the yams, the taste for breadfruit that I definitiely thought I'd lost... Or maybe it's the combination of all of it that makes me think this is the best meal I have ever had in my life. I once saw on television (the usual scene) a family of lions devouring a young antelope. When they were finished there was nothing left but white bones, without a trace of flesh left on them.

We can see the bottom of the bowl before we know it. At the same moment, a song splits the air. I can see the young man's throat swelling and deflating, like a lizard's. A formless emotion grips my heart. I feel as though I'm in another world. Somewhere far from Pétionville and its mundane concerns. The young man is leaning against a post and singing about a woman from Artibonite whose husband (Solé or Soleil or something) is gravely ill. A choir of young voices accompanies the woman in her distress. The man hovers between life and death, between night and day. But the woman is brave, she fights to save her man. Then the young man goes on to sing several folk songs that tell about the misery of peasants' lives.

Suddenly there is a sacred song: *"Papa Legba ouvri baryé pou mwen..."* I sense a new energy flowing from the choir. The girls' voices climb higher and higher, as though announcing the arrival of an eminent personage. In fact it's the Prophet, who has just appeared at the door (as the Prophet, or Legba) wearing ceremonial robes. His face is even graver than it was at our arrival. The voices reach their highest pitch and then descend slowly into silence.

"The painting is finished," the Prophet says laconically, making a sign to the young man to bring it out.

The fat woman begins to dance, although there is no music. We hear only the heavy sound of her bare heels on the ground. Suddenly she breaks into a sacred chant. A warrior's chant, although I can't make out the words. Most of them seem to be of African origin. Her flesh ripples. She scowls menacingly. The Prophet follows her with his eyes, looking vaguely disturbed. A terrible god is knocking at the door. He cannot break into our circle. Suddenly the woman slumps down in a corner, exhausted. She looks like an unstrung marionette. The audience breathes. Ogou, the terrible god of fire, couldn't spoil the party. The young man comes out carrying the Prophet's painting. It is covered with a mauve cloth. One of the young girls comes over and removes the cloth, and the magnificent but terrifying painting is revealed to us. All in mauve. The Prophet's colour. The figures and their surroundings are all mauve. All of us are in the painting. The young man, the girls in their white robes, the fat woman in mauve, the little prostitute, Carl-Henri and me. There are three figures at the centre: the Prophet in the middle, Jacques Gabriel on his left and the journalist, wearing a white wedding gown, on his right. The girl who uncovered the painting goes over to the journalist and drapes the mauve cloth over her head. All the blood has drained out of the Parisian journalist's face.

"You are witnesses to the mystical marriage of the Prophet Pierre, living and domiciled in Croix-des-Bouquets," says Jacques Gabriel in a serious and authoritative voice, "and of M.R., living and domiciled in Paris. This marriage is performed by the will of the gods, some of whom are here present."

Hysterical howling from the young girls.

SOME TIME LATER.

"No one asked me what I thought!" says the journalist, still in a state of shock.

"Voodoo gods aren't democratic," Jacques Gabriel replies, not missing a beat.

"Nevertheless, I find it scandalous."

"But if you don't believe in voodoo, it's just an amusing spectacle."

"Of course I don't believe in voodoo, whatever you . . ."

"Listen," says Gabriel, cutting her off. "You are going to return to Paris and forget what happened tonight."

"I want to go back to my hotel."

And she goes and sits in the car.

"Was it just an amusing spectacle?" I ask Carl-Henri, already half-knowing what he'll say.

"It was real. More real than anything that takes place in a church. Wherever she goes, she'll have the gods with her. She belongs to us now."

"Still," I risk, "it's a bit scary."

"On the contrary, Fanfan. Now nothing can touch her. No one can ever come up to her with the intention of hurting her. From now on she is protected. She's the wife of a very powerful member of the voodoo pantheon."

"What?" I say, astonished. "You mean it wasn't the Prophet she married?"

"No." This time it's Jacques Gabriel who answers. He is heading towards the car. "It wasn't the Prophet, it was Legba, the god who guards the border between the visible and invisible worlds."

M.R. DIDN'T SAY a word the whole way back. Neither did the little prostitute.

A Country Wedding

Magic Boys

THE OWNER OF the tiny Hibiscus Hotel had worked all his life in New York, in Brooklyn. He'd held down two jobs in factories that were at least an hour and a half from each other; he'd also owned a small bakery on Church Avenue. There are many like him, people with a dream in their heads who, in order to realize it, work like dogs in the hell that is New York. Such men and women are so obstinate that it sometimes takes thirty or more years of banging their heads against the city (New York's heart is made of granite) to knock those dreams out of them. Simply put: to stop a Haitian from dreaming, you have to beat it out of him.

The man we're concerned with now is named Mauléon Mauléus. His late father, a former judge in Gressier, left him a piece of land near the beach. He had not spent a single day in the factories without thinking about that postage stamp of land, nurturing his dream of building a small hotel, no more than a dozen rooms, nestled in the land's luxurious vegetation. As time went on he added a few huts, separate from the hotel, for clients who wanted to feel closer to nature. He'd have to bring in some white sand from Montrouis, because even though the water at the hotel was crystal clear, the sand around there was black and grey and hardly conformed to the notion of cleanliness that he associated with paradise. Blue (the sea), white (the sand), green (the countryside), those were the colours that sang of life.

And now that he has built his hotel, he doesn't have a red cent with which to hire even the small but diligent staff he would need to buy the food (fresh fish, of course) and drink for the establishment. He has been caught in this impasse now for two months. He's beginning to see nature closing back in around his hotel. Of course, there have been many who, learning of the situation, have come up to Mauléon to propose some sort of partnership deal, but he has decided he will never join up with a Haitian. His father told him often enough that when you have a Haitian for a partner one of two things can happen: either you go bankrupt within one or two years, or the Haitian will somehow arrange to have you thrown into prison while he takes over your business. "That's the way it is, that's the way it has been, and that's the way it will always be," the irascible old judge of Gressier had decreed.

Completely desperate, Mauléon has gone to see Old Sam, an American who buys up most of the small hotels in the region when they begin to experience difficulties. Sam is a red-blooded old mercenary who sold his services in many parts of the Caribbean (Jamaica, Barbados, Trinidad, the Bahamas) before settling in one of Port-au-Prince's dingier

Magic Boys

suburbs about a dozen years ago. Mauléon met him through a casino manager who owns a cottage in the area.

One day, Sam shows up at the hotel and spends the afternoon giving the place a minutely detailed inspection (the rooms, the grounds, the huts, the beach).

"The best thing you can do, Mauléon, is to get out while there's still time..."

"Why's that, Sam?"

"Look, I've owned hotels all over the Caribbean for twenty-five years, and I can tell you that a set-up like the one you've got here will do nothing but totally ruin you... I know you're a hard worker, but I don't see any possible solution..."

"What's not working?"

"Well, for one thing, it's the wrong location. The ocean is too rough in these parts... I know this business, Mauléon: you have one drowning and no one will ever come to this hotel again."

"Anything else?"

"I've been noticing a kind of strange smell since I got here... Is there a sulfur spring around here somewhere?"

"Yeah," says Mauléon, nearly inaudibly, "but I can fix that."

"Tourism is a fragile business, Mauléon... It's not something that just anyone can get into... To put it bluntly, I don't think I can work with you on this..."

"Sam, if you agree to invest in the hotel, I'm ready to split the proceeds in equal parts: half for you, and half for me..."

Sam remains thoughtful for a long moment.

"Look, I'll buy the whole thing from you outright... I'm

not in the habit of taking on partners, you see. I've always worked alone. If you're willing to sell, I'm willing to go along with it..."

"You just told me the place isn't worth anything, and now you say you want to buy it. Is there something going on here I'm not getting...?"

Silence.

"Look, Mauléon, you've gone about as far as you can go with this place, but you don't have the capital it would take to take it further. So why not let me pick up the slack?"

"Why not come in as my partner?"

Sam smiles sadly.

"Business is business, Mauléon... Sell now. In three months it won't be worth half of what I can offer you for it today..."

Mauléon's face is furious.

"This discussion is over... Whatever happens, I'll never sell the judge's land."

MAULÉON IS SITTING at the side of the road, across from the hotel, thinking things over. Of course he can always borrow more money, but then he'd have to be certain that the hotel would make a profit, and in the first year. On the other hand, there's total bankruptcy, possibly even prison. Already there are two other hotels in the vicinity that are, according to Sam, in serious trouble. But Sam, of course, is trying to panic Mauléon into selling. Maybe that's the only solution. Sell everything. But what then? Return to that hellhole, New York?

Magic Boys

No, that he will never do. But what, then? He doesn't want to move north, and he has no chance if he stays here. It's like that nightmare that has been haunting him ever since he came back to Haiti: he scrambles up a tree to escape from a tiger only to find a python sleeping in the top branches. The only thing he is sure about is that he can't hold out much longer under the present circumstances. And Sam, that old shark, will attack at the first sign of weakness and swallow him whole.

The next day Mauléon again takes up his seat on the side of the road and continues his reflections. He knows full well that the solution will have to come from his head, since he has nothing whatsoever in his pockets. Strange that he could come safe and sound from the worst jungle in the world— the Bronx, where he spent the last two years of his New York exile—only to die of boredom on the shores of Gressier. In the Bronx, one moment of inattention could earn you a bullet in the back of the head; here it's boredom that'll skin a man alive. If you have nothing to do here, you'd better invent something quick, or else long siestas, alcohol or malaria will bring you down. Mauléon is still sitting there when he notices a curious exchange taking place a hundred metres down the road: sitting on the porch of another hotel is a woman who appears to be in her fifties, sipping a coloured drink, when a young man of sixteen or seventeen crosses the sun-drenched road and approaches her table. They talk for several minutes, then the barman comes out and tells the youth to leave the porch. The young man rises politely and makes to leave, but the woman, a guest of the hotel (which is known as a gathering place for people from Quebec) says something to the barman and the young man sits back down. However, they don't stay for long. The woman empties her glass, picks up her handbag, and the two of them head off towards the beach.

Mauléon watches them for a moment as they enter the water. The woman is tall and elegant. The young man is neither particularly handsome nor well muscled. A relaxed couple. What interests Mauléon is that they didn't head straight off to one of the rooms, but went instead to the sea. The sea that knows no age. In the presence of that turquoise eternity, fifty years is not that far from seventeen. Playing in the water makes you young once more. As young as the world. Mauléon waits for a while before going over to speak to the barman. He finds the man standing on a table, changing a light bulb. He, too, is in his fifties, self-assured and a bit taken with himself.

"That couple who just left?"

Yes, of course he knows them.

"The boy came up from Port-au-Prince about two years ago. His name is Legba. He comes from the Cap, same as me. The sea puked him out one morning, and I took him in. He was as thin as a rail. I fed him, looked after him like I would any other wounded bird that washes up on the beach. That's the way I am. Every morning I ask myself what the sea is going to bring me today."

"Yes, but getting back to Legba..." says Mauléon.

"I sent him to school to learn English, which he picked up in the blink of an eye. He's a bright kid, highly intelligent.

Magic Boys

I hoped he'd continue his studies, but he went in for hard drugs and easy money, the sea, which he knows well, and forbidden fruit. I don't mind admitting that he disappoints me. That's why I don't let them hang around here. There's a whole gang of them in these parts. Mostly they come from Cité Soleil, that shantytown you can see across the bay there... They're pests..."

"And the woman?"

"She's from Quebec... When they get cold up there they come down south to get warm. It doesn't cost an arm and a leg, and every day is sunny. They come for a week or two and stay for a month, two months, even six months... And every year they come back."

"Why?"

The barman leers at him.

"Because of them," he says, pointing to a group of young men horsing around on the beach.

Mauléon watches them for a while (their young, supple bodies, their crazy laughter, their childish games). Children of the sun god. He suddenly feels as though a light has been turned on in his head. He quickly says goodbye to the barman. "That's just what I need," he tells himself when he is back on the road. He won't ban those magic boys from his hotel, he'll put up with them, he'll welcome them, he'll even invite them. They're a real gold mine.

Beach Bar

THERE THEY are, hanging around the bar down by the beach.

"A ham sandwich and a glass of pomegranate juice," Gogo calls out.

"Same for me," says Chico, "but make mine a real thick sandwich, Albert... I had a hard night last night and I need to regain my strength... Okay?"

The barman says nothing.

"Ah, don't be like that, Albert," Mario teases. "Everything'll be all right... This is better than being in jail, isn't it? Nothing to complain about... Give us a smile, just a little one... You know, I've never seen Albert smile..."

"What would you like?" Albert says to him archly.

"All right, Albert, you win. No smile today, either... So, I'll have a malted, lots of ice... I have to go up to Number Eight in a few minutes."

"Ah, you're doing Mrs. Wenner this morning!" Chico cries merrily. Chico is always in a good mood.

"She's a real hard nut to crack," says Gogo. "Hey, Albert! I said a cheese sandwich. You know I can't stand ham, it upsets my stomach... He does it on purpose, I swear..."

"Let him alone," says Mario.

"Gogo's right, Albert," Chico says, laughing. "He ordered a ham sandwich; I was there."

"Stop it, Chico," says Gogo, "you're going to drive the poor man crazy..."

"Hey, guys!" says Mario. "I've got to go up to Number Eight; someone give me some pointers... And you, Gogo, don't play the same trick on me today that you did yesterday..."

"What'd he do?" asks Chico.

"He told me that Mrs. Woodroff was a former nun and I had to fuck her from behind while saying the Lord's Prayer if I wanted to make her come..."

"Jesus! You're not even supposed to touch her," says Mario.

"She's not as bad as Mrs. Hopkins," throws in Chico, seriously, "the widow in Number Six. She spent three hours talking to me like I was her son before jumping my bones."

"I've already done her," says Gogo. "It must have been the first time in her life that she found herself alone in a room with someone who wasn't her husband."

"She must have been shy," Mario says.

"Maybe at first, but after a few minutes it was clear she knew exactly what she wanted..."

"She reminds me of Madame Bergeron," says Gogo.

"Who's that?" asks Chico.

"You remember her, the one who went around introducing herself by shouting, 'I'm Madame Bergeron from Boucherville. Do you know Boucherville?'"

"Oh, her. Now I remember," says Chico. "Why bring her up?"

"It would be like being in a restaurant with her," says Gogo, "with her giving her opinion about everything, every minute detail, making sure the meat they served was top quality, the vegetables fresh, the napkins clean, and so on."

"Oh, yeah, I remember now," says Chico, laughing. "She'd go: 'Lower, no, lower... Now higher... A little to the right... There! Now get back on, get back on, but gently, oh gently... No, my breasts, keep on massaging my breasts... Where are your hands? What are they doing? You should be using them... Now go hard, harder, as hard as you can... That's it, as hard as you can!'—she'd say that a little scornfully—'Softer... Softly... Use your tongue, too... Ah, there, now you can do what you want, I'm going to come...'"

The others watch Chico and Gogo mimicking the scene under the intensely disapproving eye of Albert.

"You can laugh if you want, Albert," says Gogo. "They won't make you pay for it, you know."

"I know he laughs," says Chico. "He's laughing on the inside. I'll bet he tells our stories to all his friends."

Albert's implacable face.

"All this talk, and I still don't know what I'm supposed to do with Mrs. Wenner. I have to go up there in a few minutes..."

"Mrs. Wenner from Cleveland, Ohio," Chico says calmly. "She's the marathoner of sex. She can go twenty-six miles without leaving her bed."

"Listen," Gogo says with a glint of panic in his eyes, "this woman is sixty years old and she can fuck without stopping for more than ten hours... Then she'll rest for ten minutes and be ready to go at it again..."

Beach Bar

"You're kidding me, Gogo..."

Gogo turns to Chico and the two of them go through a rapid dance step.

"Am I right, Chico, or am I right?"

"You're right! She's going to swallow little Mario whole in the first go-round ... *Bad deal* ..."

Gogo and Chico continue dancing, holding each other close, laughing, as though Mario's predicament is the funniest thing in the world.

"Are you going up there to Number Eight or not, Mario?" says Gogo.

"Mrs. Wenner's waiting for you, Mario," Chico teases.

"What am I going to do?" says Mario, sounding a bit frightened.

"You could go down to the Arts and Crafts Institute and learn how to do a real job, like carpentry or mechanics."

The three boys turn in perfect synchronicity towards the barman.

"Albert," says Chico, "what we do here is a real job."

"Anyway," says Gogo, "there are no dumb jobs, only dumb people. Isn't that right, Albert?"

"But what am I going to do with Mrs. Wenner?" Mario asks again.

"I know!" Chico says quickly, with his angelic smile.

"Spit it out, man," says Gogo.

"You know how after a couple of hours of fucking, she goes into a kind of trance..."

"Oh, yeah," says Gogo, "it's like she goes into automatic pilot..."

"When she's like that," says Chico, "you could get up and go for a piss and she wouldn't even notice . . ."

"Go on," says Chico.

Even Albert is listening as he sets up the bar for the afternoon cocktails.

"So, what if we do her in turns, every couple of hours?" Chico says without laughing.

"What are you saying, Chico!" cries Mario.

"It's simple enough: as soon as she goes into her own little world, one of us switches with whoever's in the room with her."

"That way," adds Gogo, "whoever's in the room can come down here to the bar and freshen up a bit, have a sandwich and a malted with extra ice, prepared by our very own games master, none other than Albert himself."

"Never mind dragging me into your filth," sniffs Albert.

"That's cool, Chico!" Gogo nearly shouts.

"But what if she dies?" asks Mario, more than a little alarmed.

"She won't die. She's got a tough old hide on her. Crocodiles like her never die under these conditions."

"They're like ants," says Chico. "Ants are never crushed by a bag of sugar."

"That's us," adds Mario. "We're the bag of sugar."

All three of them laugh. Albert pretends to wipe off the bar. Several of the hotel's female guests come into the bar area with towels wrapped around their waists and a ton of sunscreen on their faces, chests and backs. They've come up from the beach. They crowd around the bar and order their afternoon punch ("Let's put some of that heat inside us for a change!"). After three of Albert's punches everyone is pretty much settled in for the rest of the day, until at least five o'clock. There they are, standing around the bar. Those who know Albert from other hotels (Albert worked at two or three others in the area before landing at the Hibiscus) chat him up, talking fondly about the good old times. The good old days of Brise de Mer or Lambi. Albert's tone is always respectful. No familiarity with the clients, despite a few obvious come-ons from those for whom a single glass of punch makes them lose all sense of time and space. Gogo watches Albert with a strange smile on his face, a mixture of admiration and irreverence. Doesn't this guy know he's working in a brothel? People are so strange. Some people can remain the same whether they work in a church or in a bordello. Albert, for example.

"I'm going up now," Mario says suddenly.

Heading South

BRENDA

My husband and I both come from the same small town north
of Savannah. The middle of nowhere. I won't even bother telling you its name. I've never met anyone who's even seen it on
a map. I've known my husband since we were little children.
We don't come from the same religious backgrounds. He's a
Methodist and I'm a Baptist. The way I see it, it doesn't make
any difference what you call yourself as long as you believe in
God. That's what my husband told me after we got married,
and now we're both Methodists. I talk about it, anyway, but
I haven't been confirmed yet. If my husband were here, he'd
say, "That's Brenda all over!" His name is William, but he
likes to be called Bill. Actually, Big Bill. Oh, I almost forgot:
you don't have to know what to call him, because he didn't
come with me on this trip. That was my idea. I didn't think I
could ever do it, leave him alone up there like that. This isn't
the first time I've been to Port-au-Prince. It's the second. The
first time, Bill came with me. I've been wanting to come back
for two years. Pamela, I call her Pam, she's my best friend, she

says that I've been like a drug addict in withdrawal for two years. I tell her that no drug addict ever went through what I went through. My whole body suffered, my head, my chest, my blood, every possible pain you could ever imagine, I suffered. For two years. Every day. Every night. Every hour. Can you imagine such a thing? I don't think anyone who isn't called Brenda Lee, and who didn't come from a tiny little town north of Savannah, and who hasn't lived for twenty-five years with a man named Bill who hasn't touched her more than a grand total of eight times in all those years, could ever understand what I went through.

ELLEN

I've always been attracted by the South, but I never thought of coming to Port-au-Prince. As far as I was concerned, Port-au-Prince was for nymphos. Not for me. One big sex park. Anyway, I've been coming here now for five years. I come down every year and spend the whole summer. My courses end the last week of June, and generally a week later I fly to Port-au-Prince. I always stay at this hotel. It's quiet, it's clean, and it's on the beach. This is how you know you're getting old: you want everything close at hand. Port-au-Prince. Who would have guessed that this is where I would spend my holidays? I went to a private school, and for the past twenty-five years I've been teaching at Vassar. I teach stuck-up little bitches to keep their knees together so they can trap husbands. And if you think things have changed in that regard you've got one very long finger stuck like this in your eye. (She makes the gesture.) Actually, I'm supposed to be teaching contemporary literature, but all they want to know is how to go about making the best of what the good Lord gave them to work with. A tidy little mouth, two little tits that they check for signs of growth every day, blonde hair and a pretty little ass. Scrumptious little packages. And who can blame them? The boys are worse. Complete ninnies that don't deserve any better. I hate that country, even if it is my own. You can't imagine how much I loathe those little sluts and their asshole boyfriends. All they think about is getting laid and producing litters of more brats and, when they've bought as much junk as they can at their supermarkets, washing up on a beach somewhere in the Caribbean like so many overstuffed sperm whales. Always with their hair in curlers, always wearing sunglasses, always shoving their shopping carts into your legs at the checkouts. So will someone please tell me what the hell I'm doing here, where that's exactly the type of person who forms the majority? (She motions with her chin to the line of her compatriots covered in sunscreen trying to get a tan on the beach.)

SUE

I've tried every diet known to science and I still look like a blues singer from Harlem. And I've never set foot in Harlem. I never go anywhere where there's more than ten blacks. It's not that I'm afraid of blacks, it's just that black men aren't my thing. Now you're going to say that I'm not making any sense, because I'm really crazy about Neptune, and Neptune is as black as the ace of spades. But Neptune is Haitian. To me, when I say black, I mean American black. All American blacks think about is cutting white throats, and we do everything we can to help them do it. You're shocked, hearing me say that, aren't you? Well, that's what I think. Who built all those schools American blacks go to? Not them! Well, I say that, but I've also got to say that I can't stand white American males, either. They never look at a woman like me. If you want to get an American white male to notice you, you have to weigh less than a hundred and twenty pounds, and I weigh twice that. I'm still light on my feet. I work in a factory and there isn't a man there who works harder than me. I can carry a heavy box a long way. I'm strong as an elephant and light as a butterfly. If he knew how to handle me, a man could do anything he wants with me. He could make me his slave. But those idiots, all they want is some anorexic bimbo. They have no idea that under all this fat I'm as thin as a razor. Neptune is the first man who ever paid me a compliment about my weight. To him, being big isn't a fault. It's a quality. He's a fisherman. He has a little sailboat. He fishes not far from here, near the Île de la Gonâve. His philosophy is very simple: fish, eat, drink, sleep like a baby and fuck like a lion. Not a bad life, eh?

BRENDA

I'm going to tell you what happened the first time we came here, my husband and me. I wanted to wait a bit before opening up to you like this. If my husband were here, he'd say: "Brenda, you've never kept a secret longer than a day." But that's not true. There are many things about me that he doesn't know, and that he'll never know. That no one will ever know. Well, you, but it's not the same with you. I don't know you. It's good to talk like this to someone you don't know. I get the feeling you're very young to be doing this; this kind of thing requires a certain amount of experience. I'm not finding fault or anything, but back home, inspectors are usually older men. And I also don't see what use all this information will be to you. I must admit that I'm still a bit surprised, even though, as you reminded me, each country has its own ways. It's also true that people who come from rich countries tend to want to impose their ways of doing things. I apologize again for getting mixed up in things that don't concern me. I usually avoid politics like the plague... Well, to get back to my story, it all started when my husband took pity on this young man who hadn't had anything to eat for two days. A young man from Ouanaminthe, a small village in the north. You must know him, surely. His name is Legba. His mother called him that because it seems he was the first of her children to survive after six miscarriages. The name suited him. In any case, my husband asked him to join us at our table. Albert—that's the maitre d' at the hotel—he wasn't all that pleased. My husband told him that if we're paying for a room we can invite anyone we want to our table. And my husband added in a lower voice, so only Albert could hear him, that he wasn't going to let any nigger stop him from doing what he wanted. That's the way he talks, my husband, but he isn't racist or anything. In our town that's how everyone talks about black people. Anyway, Legba came over and ate with us at our table. He didn't look like he was more than fifteen years old. Right off I noticed his gleaming white teeth and his radiant smile. My husband told him he could order anything he liked. I've never seen a human being eat so much in my life. When he went to the toilet, my husband said, "He's a nice young man." Albert was still making signs to us to get rid of the boy, but my husband pretended not to notice. From the first, Legba made me think of a lost dog. Anyway, he wasn't bothering anyone, because that day we were the only guests in the dining room. But even if there had been others it wouldn't have made any difference to my husband. Methodists are like that, they'll walk all over anyone who tries to stop them from doing what they think is right. Not me, I was born Baptist. I only became a Methodist because of my husband. But in some ways I'm still a Baptist. I would have found a way to get food to Legba without offending Albert. But my husband isn't like that. Like I said, he's a Methodist. Sometimes I think people shouldn't marry outside their religion.

ELLEN

If I had my way I'd rid the Earth of everything that's dirty, and there's more of what's dirty here in this town than anywhere else I've ever been. So why, dear God, did you plant, in this dungheap, a flower as radiant as Legba? I turned fifty-five last month. I can tell you there are worse things in life. And this young man is as beautiful as a god. Do you think I could find anyone like him in Boston? Don't tell me I could because I've been in every bar in that snobbish whore of a town a hundred times, and believe me there is nothing in the North for women over forty. Nothing, nothing, nothing, you bunch of bastards!

SUE

People bring their illusions with them when they come to Port-au-Prince. Even Fat Sue. There is sun here. Fresh fruit, grilled fish, the sea.

And I have a lover.

BRENDA

My husband and I got into the habit of having every dinner with Legba. He seemed shy at first. Every night we'd spend hours talking to him about his life, his family, his future. It's like we adopted him, and he seemed to have accepted us, too. One day we suggested he join us for an afternoon on the beach. My husband knew an isolated spot. The three of us were stretched out in our bathing suits on this enormous rock, facing the sun. Legba's body fascinated me: long, supple, delicately muscled. His skin glowed. I could hardly take my eyes off him. I drank him in, trying not to be too obvious about it. It didn't take long for my husband to notice the state I was in, though, and when Legba got up to walk lankily down towards the water, my husband gave me a wink that I took as a kind of permission. When I pretended not to understand what he was on about, he told me straight out that he didn't have any objections to me giving in to my obvious inclinations. I tried to look offended, but just then Legba came back and my husband only had time to whisper, "I want you to." I

Heading South

was totally taken aback by his behaviour; it was the first time he'd ever acted like that. I completely lost my head. Legba was lying beside me on his back, with his eyes closed. I didn't dare look his way. My husband elbowed me and made me look at Legba's young, almost naked body. So I let my eyes travel over his flat, sleek stomach, his long legs, his bathing suit with its enticing mound. From then on I was in a kind of trance, hypnotized by Legba's firm yet trembling skin. I was irresistibly drawn to this body that seemed like it was being offered to me on a platter. My husband took my hand and guided it towards Legba's torso. When he let go, my hand fell on his chest and I kept it there. Legba briefly opened his eyes and then shut them again. Encouraged, I moved my hand down to his stomach. I felt an incredible thrill of pleasure travelling up from the young man's soft skin through my fingertips. My hand was trembling. I tried to stay calm but couldn't. Legba didn't move a muscle. It was as though he was making me a gift of his body. I slid two fingers under his bathing suit and took hold of his penis, which quickly began to harden in the palm of my hand so that it poked out under the string of his bathing suit. Seeing his black cock, so long, so tender, made me completely lose control of myself. My lungs were on fire. I felt waves of heat flooding between my legs. I feel awkward telling you about such an intimate experience, but believe me, it's been two years and I haven't been able to tell a soul, and yet I've relived each moment a thousand times in my head. I remember each second as though it had happened yesterday. I'm not ashamed of it anymore. I am a very sensual woman.

I hadn't known that about myself, but now I totally accept who I am. I'm a good Christian, but why else had the Good Lord put me in this degrading situation? I had absolutely no control over my desire. It was as if someone had thrown gasoline over my whole body and then lit a match. I tried, oh yes, I tried, but I couldn't stop myself. I turned into a sexual animal. Look at me—even telling you about it I'm breaking out into a sweat. (There is a long pause.) Do you want me to go on with my story? All right, but I still don't understand how it's going to help you find the man who did this. Yes, you're right, man or woman. I'm a bit lost, I'm afraid . . . Oh yes, with his arms lying by his sides, Legba was barely breathing, but regularly. I looked around quickly to see if anyone was coming our way, then I gently spread Legba's legs apart and knelt between them with my face above his penis. I took it in my mouth. I breathed up and down its length, covering it with my saliva. Then I took it into my throat as far as it would possibly go. When I couldn't stand it any longer I sat up, took off my bathing suit, and impaled myself on his rod. It tore so deep into me I couldn't hold back a howl. It felt like it was piercing me all the way up to the middle of my chest. I hadn't even recovered from the shock of it, the pain and pleasure all mixed together, before I started going up and down on him. He was breathing harder now, almost panting. But still he didn't move. My husband was lying right next to us, taking it all in. His eyes were riveted on the long, black sword that was splitting me in half. I was going faster and faster, knocking my forehead against his chest, making his cock go in farther, deeper. I think I was crying out constantly. The sight of his young body drove me even crazier. Finally I felt powerful jets of hot sperm deep inside me. They went on and on. I came, too, almost at the same time as him, completely out of my mind. I clutched at his fresh and fragile chest like a woman possessed, and jammed myself one last time on his cock, as deep as I could get it in, and held it there for a long time. He opened his eyes. He was as exhausted as I was. His eyes were red and timid and a bit frightened. Moved by a wave of gratitude, I threw myself on him, kissed him everywhere and cried like a baby. It was my first orgasm. I was fifty-five years old... I feel so tired now. Would you mind if I went and lay down for a bit...? Thank you...

ALBERT

I was born in Cap-Haïtien, in the northern part of Haiti. My grandfather was also born there. You may already know this, but my whole family fought against the Americans during the occupation of 1915. I come from a long line of patriots. My father died never having shaken a white man's hand. For him, whites were lower than monkeys. Whenever he saw a white man, he used to say, he always wanted to turn him around to see if he had a tail. My grandfather didn't even go to that much trouble. As far as he was concerned, a white man was an animal, pure and simple. He'd say "the whites," but he was talking mainly about Americans. Those who dared invade Haitian soil. The supreme insult. A slap in the face to a whole generation. I came to work in Port-au-Prince when I was twenty-two, after my father died, and got a job in this hotel right away. If my grandfather knew that his grandson was serving Americans he would die of shame. This new army of occupation isn't armed, but it has packed its suitcase with a scourge much worse than cannons: drugs. The Queen of Crimes, and she always comes with her two sidekicks: easy money and sex. There's nothing here, sir, that hasn't been touched by one or the other of these plagues. There was a time when we had morals. Now I look around me and I see that everything has come crashing down. I look at our customers, respectable women who twenty years ago, when I first started working here, would have been with their husbands. And what do I see? Lost women, animals lusting after blood and sperm. And whose fault is it? His, the master of desire. He's seventeen years old, he has eyes like glowing embers, a perfect profile. Legba: the Prince of Storms.

ELLEN
When the police found his body on the beach one morning, they immediately assumed that a drug deal had gone wrong. They didn't give a shit about the delinquents. Legba was what they call well-known to the police. He sold drugs to everyone on the beach. You don't think for one minute that the Port-au-Prince police, one of the most corrupt forces in the Caribbean, would waste time investigating the death of a young prostitute, do you? You'll have to excuse me, I'm used to saying what I think. That's why I don't really understand what you're doing. You say you work for a self-regulating department? Criminal

Investigation Services, is that what you called it? I don't know what good that can do now that Legba is dead. And I also wonder why you arc so interested in such intimate details. I know it's probably none of my business, but you're going about this inquiry in a very strange way, sir. What else do you want to know?... Yes, he was a hoodlum, but Lord, was he good looking! What's more, he knew how to make love to a woman. It's true, he could have got what he wanted just looking like a young god, and as far as I'm concerned that would have been enough to make me happy. I could have spent hours just looking at him. He could do whatever he wanted with me. And in that he was indefatigable. I mean, think about it: I spent eighteen years in the best universities in the States learning the best ways of improving my quality of life on this planet, and all that time all I really needed was an adolescent here in Port-au-Prince. He played my body like a guitar, and believe me, he knew how to handle his instrument. There were times when I thought I was going to die, I kid you not. My body felt completely drained, as though he'd pumped everything out of it. He could bring me to orgasm almost without touching me. Me, who had always intimidated American men, who are supposed to be the most powerful men in the world, at least in terms of economic and political power, and here I was completely in thrall to a boy in Port-au-Prince. With him I was no longer Ellen the Cynic, I was a little twit who wanted nothing more than to be touched in the right places. And he knew them all, by instinct. The first time I laid eyes on him, down by the hotel, I was afraid of making a fool of myself; after all,

I was in my fifties. And I wet myself. I had to go up to my room to change. I stood in front of my mirror and masturbated, thinking about him. He had such an insolent mouth, and my God did I want that mouth. I dreamed about him caressing me with his hands so often that when he finally did touch me it was like we'd always been lovers. But what I wanted most, what gave me the highest orgasms, was to have his long, fine penis in my mouth. I would wake up in a sweat in the middle of the night. By day it was different, I could be Ellen the Cynic, able to thumb my nose at the rest of the world. My punching bag at the time was that fatty, Sue. I didn't care at all that she was fat, but I could never understand why she would choose Neptune when Legba was available. I didn't understand it then, and I don't understand it now. How could she not get down on her knees before such a black sun? To me, anyone who feels nothing in the presence of such beauty is dangerous. Of course, if she had once dared to look at Legba I would have scratched her eyes out.

ALBERT

One day I came upon them by the stairs. She was hanging on his neck and complaining that he was driving her crazy. You know who I'm talking about? That intellectual from Boston, the one with her nose always up in the air. Legba wasn't saying a word, as usual. His face was blank. He knew how to drive that kind of woman around the bend. She was crying like a teenager who'd just lost her first love. Yes, sir, as I've always said, it's the cynics who are the hardest hit.

Heading South

BRENDA

I always try to speak well of people, but since you asked me what I truly think, I have to admit that Ellen isn't a woman, she's a bitch in heat playing at being an intellectual. She was lost the moment she first laid eyes on Legba. Really, it was disgusting to watch. People like her don't know the difference between sex and love.

SUE

It's true, Brenda is very discreet. She's not one of those women who show their emotions. Her face is always calm. I would never have known what she was going through if she hadn't confided in me. That day she seemed totally lost. I'd never seen her like that. She came into my room, which she'd never done before, and she said: "I can't do it anymore, Sue. I think I'm going to kill him, and then kill myself." Coming from Brenda, I didn't know what to think. I didn't even know who she was talking about. I vaguely thought she was talking about her husband, because I knew they weren't getting along very well. I thought that that was why she'd come down here on her own this time. That's what I thought, anyway. Until she admitted to me that she was in love with Legba. How a woman like Brenda, who is so serious, such a devout Christian, could fall in love with a little gigolo like him was beyond me. He acted like a prince because this German woman had given him a gold chain that he wore around his neck like a leash. A pitiful little drug dealer. Surely you know he sold cocaine on the beach? Since his death the other young prostitutes have vanished into the woodwork. I haven't seen one of them on the beach. Gogo, Chico, not even the handsome one, Mario. All gone off somewhere, like a cloud of flies attracted by the smell of a fresh corpse. Anyway, when Brenda came out and told me point blank that she was in love with the little rat I had the surprise of my life. But there's no point going on about it. People's feelings are part of life's impenetrable mysteries, I must have read that somewhere. Oh, I stopped wondering about life a long time ago. I take things as they come. Brenda told me that Legba had stopped coming to their rendezvous, and she couldn't stand the pain of it any longer. She couldn't sleep, she couldn't eat. All she could think of was him. And he couldn't care less about her. The only thing he was interested in was money. She spent the whole day in her room, she said, bawling her eyes out under a pillow. She couldn't go on living like that. She was talking quietly, sometimes so low I couldn't understand half of what she was saying. Just saying his name, over and over. "Such pain," I thought. There's nothing I can do for her. She's the only one who can control her destiny. That's just the way it is. I suggested she take some tranquilizers, and she just looked at me in alarm, and I knew she'd already tried that. That's when I realized that if Brenda was confiding in me it could only mean one thing: she wanted me to stop her from committing a crime. Of that I am certain.

ELLEN

I love love so much—love or sex, I don't know which anymore—that I've always told myself that when I'm old I'll pay

Heading South

to get it. I just didn't think it would happen so soon. That boy was Satan personified. The Prince of Light. But the kind of light that can kill you. He showed me what hell was like. I'd never been afraid of suffering, but this was too much. I'd given him everything. In return, he'd humiliated me in ways I'd never imagined possible. He dragged me through the mud. I took it all. It makes me laugh, now, the way Brenda goes around acting like the weeping widow. I'm the widow. Brenda couldn't have known a hundredth part of what I had to put up with just to be near him. The flames of hell. Imagine a young, arrogant kid like he could be, with a woman of my age. Can you even imagine what it would be like with him and his friends? There's Ellen Graham, the hag. But time heals all wounds. Brenda spends her days in her room, crying. Me, I don't cry.

SUE

It's a terrible thing to say, but I'm sure it was either Ellen or Brenda who killed him. He drove them to it, them and others, too, and what was bound to happen one day happened. All because of the contempt that northern men have for women of their own race.

ALBERT

That morning I went to see a friend who works at a small hotel not far from here. When I came back, I walked along the beach. It was dawn. The beach was empty except for someone who looked as though he'd spent the night there. As I got closer I could see it was Legba. He looked like a sleeping angel, curled up on the sand like that. His face in complete repose. When I reached him it seemed to me that the night had been pretty rough on him. But even then all I saw was a frail young man. He even looked like he was smiling. I don't know why, but I sat down beside him. There was no one else on the beach. There was that strange dawn light. The feeling of being nowhere. I began to stroke his hair. He shivered as though he was cold. I lay down beside him and took him in my arms. I can't tell you how bizarre it all seems to me now. It was like I was watching my double. I remember that light in my eyes. That music in my head. That young body on the beach, almost naked. And no one else about. "Careful," I told myself, "beware of the sweetness of this skin." And I... kissed him. I kissed Legba. It was the first time I'd ever kissed a man. I kissed him. Everywhere. He responded to my caresses in his sleep, I think it was probably out of habit. I should have got up and run away, but it was too late. I was already caught up in the fiery ring of desire. I hadn't known that such physical happiness could exist. That morning I ate of the fruit of the tree of good and evil. Strange, isn't it, that without even asking me any questions you've made me bring up all the secrets that I kept hidden in the deepest recesses of my being.

ELLEN

Well, he certainly hid his light, didn't he, the hypocrite! Every time I went out looking for Legba I'd get this mean look from him... Because he was a rival. I wanted to go up to him and slap him in the face. I can tolerate anything but bigotry. Always with his nose stuck in the Bible, the little shit-arse! Now that he's got a taste for it, as he says, he's not going to switch to another road. I don't believe a word of what he told you: the dawn, the light, the music of the spheres, the forbidden fruit, it's all just shit in a silk stocking. Oh sure, once it was over he had to rush off and do his penance. I'd like to have seen him whipping himself. He's the worst kind of sadist. And let me tell you something: that's the kind that can kill.

BRENDA

Of course I can't go home. I don't have a home anymore, or a husband. I don't want to have anything more to do with northern men. I'd like to spend time on other Caribbean islands. Cuba, Guadeloupe, Barbados, Martinique, Dominica, Jamaica, Trinidad, the Bahamas... They all have such pretty names. I want to get to know them all.

The Network
(A Screenplay)

INTERIOR BEDROOM. 9:30 AM

Tanya (petite, sexy, brunette) wakes up. She stretches luxuriously in her bed. The telephone rings.

"Hello?" (*Tanya's sleepy voice.*) "It doesn't matter, I was already awake. Who's this?"

"Guess."

"Ah, it's you, Simone... What's up?"

"I got home at six o'clock in the morning..."

"I was so tired last night I thought I'd die of exhaustion. Don't you ever feel like that?"

"You know how paranoid I am, Tanya. I think I'm dying every five minutes. Sometimes I even see myself lying in a coffin."

"Well, listen to this: here I was, all dressed, makeup on and everything, and just before going out I pour myself my usual glass of rum, no ice, and, you won't believe this, but I took one sip, one single, solitary sip, and fell back on the bed like I was stone cold dead... it was a complete blackout, Simone."

"When you hadn't shown up by two in the morning I went looking for you... Your house was totally dark."

"Why didn't you come in? You have a key! I was here!" (*She laughs.*)

"Because there's always a light on at your place. Even when you go to bed you leave the television on. But last night, nothing, complete darkness…I thought maybe you'd gone out with someone." (*Nervous laughter.*)

"You mean Fanfan? Don't be silly! His type doesn't interest me one bit. You don't have to believe me if you don't want to, but I was here, Simone. Dead to the world. A complete blackout, like I said. Nothing. Total vacuum."

"Well, you missed a good time, Tanya. Tabou outdid themselves last night, a real mess. They had a contract for eight thousand dollars, half at ten o'clock and the other half at midnight. Well, Tabou didn't start playing until one o'clock in the morning. The owner of the nightclub, you know Freddy, he refused to give them the second half of the money. So Tabou only played until three and then quit. Well, the crowd tore the place apart. They smashed chairs and tables, everything they could get their hands on."

"Tabou only played for two hours! That's crazy! Why would they do that? Freddy's always been good to them."

"I don't really know what went on…It was a crazy night. At around four, Harry took us to a diner out on the airport road to get something to eat…"

"Harry Delva!?"

"Harry Delva's gone, sweetie. He's got the shakes in some freezing basement apartment in Boston. Coke's made him as thin as a rail. He sleeps with his guitar, which is the only thing he has left… No, I'm talking about the American consul…"

"Oh, that Harry... He scares me. He's got the eyes of a serial killer... But why didn't you go to Pétionville?"

"We did, but get this: everything was closed!"

"What do you mean, closed? I thought Kane's..."

"You know that Minouche and Kane... Anyway, let me finish my story. So, Harry parked the car in a swamp, and I lost a shoe in the mud."

"Oh, I wish I'd been there!"

Tanya is doubled up on the bed, a hoarse laugh escaping from her chest.

"Go ahead, laugh, but it was a nightmare. A total nightmare. I spent the rest of the night with one shoe. And to top it all off, I've never had a worse meal in my life. It was so dark in there I couldn't see my hand in front of me. I mean, I couldn't even tell you what I was eating."

Tanya is rolling about on the bed, twisted in the silk sheets. The telephone slips from her hand.

"I can't believe I missed it!"

"Not to mention the mosquitoes!"

"Stop, stop, Simone, let me catch my breath!"

"I'm telling you it was a nightmare, and all you can do is laugh... You think it's funny!"

"Don't be mad at me, Simone, please. It'll pass. I wasn't laughing at you..."

Simone seems genuinely upset.

"I have to hang up now, Tanya. I haven't slept yet."

"I'm sorry, my sweet, I didn't mean to—"

Click.

The Network

Tanya is sitting on her bed, applying nail polish (fingers and toes). The telephone rings.

"Hello..."

"It's Minouche! Is this a bad time? Anyway, it doesn't matter...Where were you last night? You missed everything, you poor dear. Freddy got into a big fight with the boys from Tabou."

"Oh?"

"Something about their contract. Anyway, it doesn't matter... Oh, my dear, it was superb. Everyone was there except you. Alta hasn't told you anything about it? You know what a mean tongue she has, she told everyone that you weren't there because Fanfan wouldn't let you go out..."

"No one tells me where I can and cannot go, you hear me, Minouche? And certainly not that pitiful little shit, Fanfan. I go where I like."

"Don't yell like that, Tanya! I couldn't care less about Fanfan, my poor dear; I don't understand for a minute what it is you see in him... Anyway, it was a perfectly nutty evening. What about you, are you all right?"

"Of course I'm all right. Why are you asking me that?"

"Don't tell anyone it was me who told you this, but last night Simone let it slip that you tried to commit suicide."

"She said *what?*"

"You know what she's like, that Simone, when she gets on her holier-than-thou kick. Sometimes I want to punch her pretty little face in. I don't understand why you clasp that vicious little snake to your bosom."

"Let's not go into all that again, Minouche."

"You're still defending her! Anyway, it doesn't matter..."

"So let's drop it, then, shall we?"

Long silence (stalemate).

"All right. She said she went out to look for you at about one o'clock in the morning, and found your house in total darkness. And since she has a key, which is something I don't have, despite our ten years of friendship..."

"Never mind that, Minouche... go on with your story."

"Since she has a key, as she never misses an opportunity to remind me... No, really, Tanya, why did you give that little bitch a key when you won't even let your best friend into your house?"

"Can't you guess, Minouche?"

"Tanya, don't tell me you're still mad at me for borrowing a couple of dresses, what was it, five years ago?"

"And all my jewelry, and a dozen pairs of almost new shoes, and eleven evening gowns... That's not borrowing, Minouche, that's moving me out. So please, go on with your story."

"Very well, since you refuse to let that little incident go... Your friend Simone, who has a key to your house, let herself in and found everything strewn all over the place, which is not like you at all. At first she thought thieves had broken in. But no, it wasn't that, because everything was there, nothing had been stolen. Then she saw a green pill bottle on the bed. She started screaming, and a woman, your downstairs neighbour, apparently, came in and told her that an ambulance had just left, with you in it."

The Network

Long silence.

"Are you still there, Tanya?"

"So what do you think happened, Minouche? That I tried to commit suicide last night, that an ambulance came and everything, that they had to pump my stomach with a rubber tube, and that I'm here, now, talking to you, fresh as a daisy... Is that what you think?"

"Well, fortunately we didn't go to the hospital. Everyone wanted to, you know. Can you imagine, all of us descending on the hospital in at least five cars. It was Fanfan who said no. He said it was just you and your histrionics, and he wasn't interested in taking part in it."

Brief silence.

"He said that?" Tanya asked, her voice flat.

"So we stayed at the club. Where Tabou, let me tell you, dear, outdid themselves. A total mess, but it doesn't matter..."

"Was Fanfan with someone last night?"

"Listen, my dear, I wasn't paying attention... He's a little shit, you know, and I've got better things to do. Are you sure you're all right?"

"Yes, I'm fine... It's not the end of the world, missing a night of listening to Tabou."

"No, of course not. So if you're sure you're all right, I'll go. I just called to see how you were. You know, I've been a bit worried about you for some time, now... You shouldn't pay so much attention to that little shithead, Fanfan. Anyway, at one point in the evening I saw him with Alta."

"That slut!"

"Take it easy, Tanya. I'll call you again this evening. Carole's going to pick me up in a few minutes."

"Where are you going?"

"To Kyona Beach. I'll call again later."

INTERIOR KITCHEN. 11:23 AM

Tanya is eating a bowl of strawberries and yoghurt. The telephone rings.

"How are you, my dear?" (*Serious voice.*)

"Listen, Alta, if you want to know whether or not I'm still alive, the answer is yes, and I'm doing just fine, thank you."

"Why are you speaking to me like that?"

"Let me tell you a few things, Alta, just so you'll know. First, I am not going out with Fanfan, because I am not accustomed, as you are, to robbing the cradle... Let's just say I sleep with him from time to time, and that it doesn't bother me in the least if you do, too..."

"Are you crazy or what? I call simply to find out if you're all right, and you jump down my throat. Tanya, you're becoming a real paranoid. What makes you think I have any interest in Fanfan? He's not my type, believe me."

"Then why did you tell everyone that Fanfan never lets me go anywhere?"

"I said that?"

"Yes, you did."

"Well, I might have said something like that... Anyway, it's true... I've never understood what you see in him. At first it was kind of cute, Tanya and Fanfan. But now, my dear, you're making a laughing stock of yourself, being jealous over a man who sleeps with everyone."

"Who told you I was jealous over Fanfan?"

"Oh, stop it, Tanya, you're being ridiculous... Apparently you tried to commit suicide last night. In any case, that's what everyone is talking about."

Click

INTERIOR LIVING ROOM. 1:05 PM
Tanya is feeding her goldfish. The telephone rings.

"Hello."

"It's me, Simone."

"So, I hear you told everyone I tried to commit suicide last night."

"I never said that, Tanya... I knew Minouche would go around saying something like that, that little snake! You know how jealous she is of our friendship."

"Except for you, Simone, no one could know what happened... You must have come in here last night, found the apartment empty, and gone downstairs to talk to my neighbour, who told you that an ambulance had been here."

"No, I did not go downstairs to question your neighbour... She came up."

"I knew it, Simone... I knew you were a nosy little snoop. Minouche may be a thief, but she's not a liar. You know how much I hate sneaky people, Simone, you know that about me. I'd rather have a thief for a friend than a sneak. So I want my key back. I want you to bring it to me this very day."

"Why are you treating me like this, Tanya?"

"You know what I'm like, Simone. When someone is my friend, they can take anything they want from me, anything. Everything I have is hers. All I ask in return is that she doesn't lie to me..."

"But you tell lies all the time, Tanya. I don't understand you..."

"I can tell lies if I want to, but nobody else can. That's just the way it is."

"Why are you being like this?" (She is crying.) "You know how much I love you...I can't live without you, my darling... Why are you treating me like this?"

"I warned you, Simone."

"Don't let me go, Tanya." (She is spluttering.) "You're the only person who understands me. You're my mother, my sister, my lover. I love you, darling. I've never loved anyone the way I love you."

"Then why do you continue to lie to me?"

"I'm not lying, Tanya...My love, I'm telling you the truth. It's you I love. I love the way you love me. You're the only one who can give me an orgasm, I swear. My body is yours whenever and however you want it, my dearest love..."

"Come here now."

"I'm still in bed, Tanya...I'll come around five this afternoon, is that all right?"

"You're a liar."

"I want you, Tanya."

"Then why won't you come right away?"

"Because I haven't had any sleep, my dearest."

The Network

"No, I'll tell you the real reason... It's because you have someone there with you now."

"No, I'm here alone."

"If you tell me one more lie, you won't even have to bring me my key. I'll have the locks changed."

"All right, yes," (she murmurs), "there's someone here...He's taking a shower."

"Who is it?"

"Just someone I met last night."

"What's his name?"

"You don't know him."

"I'm going to count to three, Simone. One... Two... Three..."

"Fanfan."

"You slut!"

"He was too drunk to go home. He asked me if he could sleep at my house."

"Simone—"

"What?"

"You do what you want. You can sleep with a donkey, for all I care, but never, never insult my intelligence. Do you understand?"

"All right... But we haven't done anything yet. He just went in to take a shower."

"Leave while he's taking his shower, come here now."

"Do you think?"

"It's up to you. I can always call Minouche."

"I'll be there, Tanya."

Tanya and Simone are in bed.

"Fanfan means nothing to me, you know that."

"Then what's he doing in your house?"

"It's your own fault, Tanya."

"Meaning what?"

"You make me so jealous I get crazy, sometimes . . . I wanted to sleep with him just so I could know what you see in him."

Tanya smiles. Simone is the one who introduced her to Fanfan. At the time, she was sharing Fanfan with Minouche. There had been almost daily fights.

"He's just a man, Simone. Nothing more or less. He's available when I feel like a fuck, that's all."

"I don't believe you, Tanya. That guy has driven you nuts. Ever since you met him you haven't been the same. I think it's very simple, what you do, Tanya. You sleep with us, and by 'us' I mean Minouche, Carole, Marie-Flore, even Alta, but you really only give yourself to men. You play with us, but it's only men who can hurt you."

"What do you mean by that?"

"What I just said doesn't change our situation. You know you don't have to worry about me. It's simple: you can have me whenever you want me. So let's talk about something else . . ."

"No, no, Simone. I want to get this straight . . ."

"But it's already clear, my love. None of us could ever get you as worked up as you are about Fanfan. For the past month you've neglected everyone but him, but in fact it could just as well have been any man. You get on top for us, but you go down on your back for a man. Even I can see that, Tanya. So you see, everyone knows what's up with you."

A long silence.

"It's true that sometimes I feel like a man."

"With us, Tanya. But whenever there's a man in the house you turn into the worst kind of woman."

"You've noticed that?"

"A child could see that, Tanya."

"There no man in the house now, Simone..."

Tanya leans over Simone and kisses her long and skilfully.

"Oh, Tanya... Do what you like with me..."

INTERIOR BEDROOM. 7:13 PM

Tanya and Simone are still in bed. Tanya gets up quietly. Simone is still sleeping. Tanya carefully picks up the telephone and takes it to the other side of the room. She dials a number.

"Hello..."

"Is Simone there?" Tanya asks, watching Simone asleep in her bed.

"No, she went out."

"Is that you, Fanfan?"

"Who's this?"

"Tanya."

"Tanya, don't hang up, please, I can explain about last night. In the end I didn't go out at all. I had one hell of a headache, my sweet."

"Did you take that medicine I bought for you the other day?"

"No, I couldn't find the bottle."

"But my love, you aren't well. That's why I keep buying you medicine. What are you doing at Simone's?"

"Nothing. I just dropped by to pick up a sweater that Charlie left here a few days ago, and I saw she wasn't home, so..."

While talking to Fanfan, Tanya stretches out her right foot and lightly runs her toes up and down Simone's firm, well-rounded bottom.

"Are you going to wait for her?"

"No, I'm leaving now."

"Don't leave yet, my love. I'll get a taxi and be there in five minutes."

Tanya gets up cautiously so as not to awaken Simone. She goes into the bathroom, takes a shower, then puts on a short dress and leaves her apartment by the back entrance.

In her sleep, Simone smiles.

A New Girl

TANYA COMES IN shortly after midnight with a cigarette in her hand (its filter smeared with lipstick). The huge dance floor at the Cabane Créole is already full to bursting. The Tabou Combo is exploding on a stage decidedly too small for the group. The musicians seem to be in top form. "That's thunder," as Freddy says when he's had too much to drink. Each table has its own bottle of cognac. Rum is for the plebes. As always, when she feels the physical pleasure of it rise within her, Tanya begins to laugh to herself. She stands in an advantageous spot and scans the room carefully before crossing to the best table. She waits for the right moment to cross the room. A pause. She puts out her cigarette. Now she goes. Shoubou (the combo's singer since the heroic epoch of Bébé Paramount), an old friend, sees her and announces her presence over the mike:

"And here we have the lovely Tanya. She is beautiful, she is beautiful, beeee-youuuu-teeee-full..."

Tanya smiles.

"Tanya!"

She turns towards Minouche, who is sitting by the stage.

"I didn't think I'd see you here tonight, Tanya..."

"Why not? I go out when I want to."

"I didn't mean to make you angry, my dear."

"Save your breath, then."

"Unwind, Tanya... I just wanted to warn you."

"Warn me about what?"

"I was just saying..."

"If you have something to say, Minouche, spit it out. I don't have all day."

"Sorry, but I thought you knew."

"So you don't have anything to say," Tanya says, and continues on her way.

ALTA CATCHES TANYA near the washrooms.

"I didn't think you'd be here tonight, Tanya..."

"Jesus! You, too, Alta?

"Fanfan is here."

"What's that got to do with me?"

"He's with a girl."

"Alta, Fanfan is always with a girl. That's not the end of the world for me."

"Oh, I see."

"That's all, Alta. Mind your own business from now on."

"Thank you, my dear."

Tanya is still sitting in a cubicle in the ladies' room, her head in her hands, when two girls come in.

"Do you think she's beautiful?" asks the first.

"Who?" replies the other.

A New Girl

"Tanya."

"Oh. She's not bad, but I think Shoubou was exaggerating."

"I think her type is a bit passé . . ."

"What type is that?"

"The kind with a flower behind her ear."

"I think she has nice eyes, but I don't like her hands."

"You noticed them, too?"

"So what was Shoubou going on about, then?"

"Didn't you figure it out? He was warning Fanfan that Tanya had come in. Those two share everything."

"What do you mean?"

"You know what I mean."

"No, I don't . . ."

"Seriously? Well, it's simple. If Shoubou has a girl, she has to sleep with Fanfan, too, and vice versa . . ."

"How do you know?"

"Alta told me."

"I didn't know Alta went with Shoubou."

"Not with Shoubou; with Fanfan."

"Oh, okay, that doesn't surprise me. He hits on anything that moves."

"And he seldom misses," the second girl sneers.

They leave.

TANYA WANTS TO see what the girl with Fanfan looks like. She's a beauty. Tall, thin, sophisticated, whereas she, Tanya, is short, sexy and common. Quite a match!

"Hey, Fanfan."

"Hey, Tanya."

"I haven't see much of you lately."

"I had some business to finish up with Shoubou."

"A girl."

"What?"

"I said, you had some girl to finish up with Shoubou... I hear you two are quite the team."

"I don't see where you're going with that..."

"Forget it, Fanfan. Aren't you going to introduce me to your friend?"

"Michèle, this is Tanya."

"Oh, yes. I've been hearing a lot about you, Tanya..."

"I'll bet you neglected to tell her that I'm one of your mistresses, Fanfan. How many of us are there, here? Do you even bother to count anymore?"

"Don't be vulgar, Tanya."

"That must be the new you, Fanfan. You used to like them vulgar, if I'm not mistaken. What's your specialty? Blow jobs?"

"Excuse me?"

Not a muscle moves on Fanfan's face.

"You must be new around here."

"I've only just met Fanfan."

"So, he hasn't told you about Shoubou yet, then? Do you like sandwiches?"

"I... I don't know what you mean."

"What are you waiting for, Fanfan? You're getting old, my dear. Cat got your tongue? You'd like me to leave? I'm sorry if I've spoiled your evening, my dear... I'll just go tell Shoubou to get ready, since it seems he'll be having 'some business to finish up' later this evening... Ciao, Michèle."

"Goodbye, Tanya."

Tanya turns back.

"And so polite, too... Tell me, Fanfan, where'd you dig up this rare gem? Are you cruising the convents, now? Oh, I get it, you found her at Madame Saint-Pierre's school. I recognize the type. I wonder if she knows you're also sleeping with Madame Saint-Pierre?"

IN SHOUBOU'S dressing room.

"You dried-up piece of shit!"

"What's the problem, Tanya?"

"You faggot!"

"Are you going to tell me what it is I seem to have done?"

"I thought you were my friend. Why didn't you call me to warn me? I would never have come here..."

"You know how it is with Fanfan... I never saw this girl before an hour ago, sitting alone at a table... Everyone was gawking at her, all the guys homing in on her. She was obviously waiting for someone. Even Charlie came up and asked who she was. I couldn't tell him a thing. No one's ever seen her before. Fanfan came in a couple of minutes before you did. I didn't have time to call you."

A long moment of truce.

"I was in the washroom and overheard two women talking about you and Fanfan. They said you shared women..."

"Tanya, dearest..."

"Don't you dare come near me."

"But Tanya, you've been had. By Maryse."

"What's Maryse done?"

"She sent those two girls into the washroom. They were sitting at her table... What's the matter, Tanya?"

"Oh, no, no, no, you're not going to get off that easily..."

"Why, have you two already slept together?"

"Are you serious?"

"You're a better judge of him than those two girls, Tanya..."

"Shit, Shoubou... Why does he treat me like this?"

"Give him a taste of his own medicine."

"With you, I suppose?"

"Why not?"

She pounces on him with claws exposed.

"You pig!"

"Stop it, Tanya... I was kidding... Jesus! What's got into you? I remember when Fanfan and I first met you, at that carnival at the Ibo Lélé Hotel, remember? Fanfan fell head over heels for you. He said you were his soulmate. You drank, you picked up men, and when they no longer interested you, you tossed them on the rubbish heap. Fanfan loved that about you. 'My friend,' I said to him, 'that one there is different, you won't be able to treat her like the rest of them.' And he nodded... And now look at you, you're acting exactly like all the rest..."

Silence.

"I could have any man I want in this city."

"So what's the problem?"

"Except him."

A New Girl

"I never looked at it like that before . . . I'm sorry, Tanya."

"What should I do now?"

"Go home."

"Everyone will think I'm afraid of that girl."

"You know as well as I do that you can't win with a new girl."

"What if I stayed?"

"It's up to you."

"What does that mean?"

"It means I'm not getting mixed up in it."

"All right. But I'm not going to go out there and walk across the whole room . . ."

"No, you can go out the back way . . . I have to go back on stage. I'll send Chérubin, he'll see you home. That way no one will know you're gone . . ."

"Anyway, I don't want to see anyone for a week, not even him . . ."

"Don't worry, you won't see him."

"Pig!"

There is the sound of applause and shouting.

"I have to go, Tanya . . . He'll come back to you, Tanya. He always comes back to you."

"I don't know anymore . . ."

"That's what you always say . . ."

SHOUBOU CLIMBS UP on the stage. The crowd yells. As he walks up to the microphone, he gives Fanfan a discreet but reassuring wink. This isn't the first time he's got his friend out of a jam. But the new girl looks very nice. Stay tuned.

A Fishing Trip

SITTING AT THE counter in the Quiesqueya, Tanya orders a cognac.

"How'd it go last night?" asks the bartender.

"I didn't stay... I was totally wiped. I went home and was in bed by midnight. Fanfan was exhausted, too. I fell asleep fully dressed."

"And now?"

"Oh, I'm perfectly rested now."

The bartender moves to the other end of the counter to serve a customer, a white man with a tall, well-built woman. You couldn't really call them breasts. They were more like grenades.

"Who's the guy?" Tanya asks idly.

"He's the American consul... A good customer... He hits on everyone who has a nice ass like yours, or breasts like hers... You know what I mean? I find the girl he's with a lot more interesting. She's superb."

"Not bad."

"You call that 'not bad'? You want me to introduce you to the guy? It could be arranged, you know..."

"Not right now ... I wonder what you see in her. She's not as pretty as all that ..."

"Maybe not, Tanya, but have you not noticed her breasts?"

"It's stupid. Every man I know is completely obsessed with breasts."

"I can't speak for all men," says the bartender, wiping a small puddle of water off the counter, "but for me, breasts drive me crazy."

"Ah, now I get it," says Tanya, giving a small laugh. "You want me to leave with the guy so you can console his girlfriend."

The bartender chuckles.

"It's all about self-interest. You want another cognac? On the house ..."

He pours her a drink. Tanya stares at the liquid in the glass for a long time. The American has just noticed her presence. He's given her a brief but intense look. The kind of look that takes everything in. Everything that can possibly be discerned about her, absorbed in a second. Tanya (petite, brunette) is not an earth-shattering beauty. You may not even notice her when she first walks into a room (unlike Simone or Minouche, if you like that type). But anyone who does check her out, even once, cannot refrain from giving her a second look. And a third. And a fourth. Why is this? A special sensuality that informs her skin, her way of moving her body (as though she never stops dancing), and, above all, her eyes. Ah, Tanya's eyes. Her favourite weapon. When she deigns to turn them your way (with a look that is both sweeping and focused at the same time), you want to hide under the table.

Everything she does she does slowly, but with incredible energy! At the moment she has just fired three salvoes at the consul, sitting at the far end of the counter. And here he is, on his way over.

"Can I buy you a drink?"

"You're with someone, I believe..."

"That doesn't stop me from being able to buy you a drink."

"Possibly not, but for your information, I'm not a whore, as you apparently think I am... Is that how you regard all Haitian women?"

The American backs off slightly.

"I've never thought any such thing..."

"Then why are you so intent on buying me a drink? Do you think I'm too poor to pay for my own drinks?"

"It was just a spontaneous gesture... I'm like that... My name is Harry, I'm the American consul."

"When you are with someone, the polite thing to do is to stay with her..."

"You're right," Harry says brusquely. Everything about him is brusque. He turns and goes back to his seat.

A moment later, the bartender speaks to her. "You practically chased the guy away. I thought you were interested in him."

Tanya's ambiguous smile.

"What makes you think I'm not?"

"You just kicked his ass for him."

"It was either his or mine."

The bartender makes a gesture as though to say he gives up.

"You women, you're all impossible. Totally impossible."

A Fishing Trip

"We simply need to defend ourselves," she says, whimpering slightly.

"When you want someone you're capable of crawling two hundred kilometres on your hands and knees to get to him. But if we take a single step in your direction, out come the claws."

"That's the way it is, Papa."

"Don't call me Papa."

"Okay, Papa."

He smiles.

"Don't you want another cognac?"

"I do. And give him the bill," she says, pointing to Harry.

The bartender's jaw drops.

"Okay, now I don't get it. You just refused to let him buy you a drink..."

Tanya waves her hand as though brushing away an imaginary fly.

"Don't worry, he'll pay. He likes paying for things."

"Whatever you say. If he doesn't, I'll cover it myself."

"Thanks, Papa, but I don't want your money. I know he'll pay."

The young woman with the dangerous breasts gets up and heads for the washroom, taking her purse with her, which suggests she'll be in there for a while. Tanya waits a moment (long enough to calmly finish her cognac) before following her.

TANYA FINDS HER crying in front of the mirror.

"What's the matter?" Tanya asks sympathetically.

The woman hides her face in her hands.

"He's all yours. You can have him . . ."

"Who?"

"Don't make fun of me, on top of everything else. Do you think it's fun talking to a man who can't take his eyes off another woman?"

"No, I don't. But I haven't laid a finger on your man."

"That's why I'm giving him to you."

"But I don't want him . . ."

The young woman suddenly begins to sob so energetically her breasts bounce up and down as though she's riding a bicycle down a bumpy street.

"You drove him crazy."

The two women look at each other in silence.

"What if I tell you it's you I'm interested in," says Tanya, calmly.

"What?"

"Don't worry," Tanya adds reassuringly. "All I meant was that you touch me, deeply."

"Thanks," says the young woman, lowering her eyes modestly.

"Tanya. And you?"

"I'm Florence."

"Florence, I'm going to make you a proposal," Tanya says brightly.

The young woman looks up quickly.

"What kind of proposal?"

"How about you and I leave him sitting there, high and dry. We'll go get a drink somewhere else . . . Don't worry, you never lose a man by dumping him."

A Fishing Trip

A pause. Then the young woman smiles. Tanya smiles, too.

"Okay. Let's leave him there...Let's go somewhere else."

"Come on," Tanya says. "That way. I know another way out."

"Where are we going?"

"We'll go to the Hippopotamus. But first I have to stop at my place. It won't take long."

"Is it far?"

"No, it's just across the way...Whenever I get bored I come here to chat up the bartender. He's very nice."

"Is he your boyfriend?" Florence asks, naïvely.

"My boyfriends are never nice...The nice ones are only my friends."

"Too bad for you..."

Tanya smiles.

"I like it that way. What about you?"

"Me?" says Florence, a little off balance. "I don't know...I don't know..."

"Still trying to find yourself?"

"I guess so," says Florence with a dry laugh.

"Well, we'll have a drink, and your little fit of depression will just disappear. You'll see."

"DARLING!" TANYA CALLS as she walks into the house. "Are you here?"

No reply.

"Where are you, darling?"

"In the bedroom."

Tanya turns to Florence, who is standing by the door.

"Have a seat for a moment. I'll be right back..."

She hurries into the bedroom.

"What are you doing, my dearest? Still sleeping?"

"Get off my back, Tanya."

"I went out for a drink, darling, while you were sleeping, and you'll never guess what I've brought you."

"Not another bottle of bloody perfume, I hope. I didn't even know they sold that shit in the bars around here..."

"Don't make fun of me, my love. Tell me this: who, in your opinion, is tall, svelte, has lots of hair and the biggest pair of tits you ever saw?"

Fanfan sits up immediately.

"She's here?"

"And she's all yours, if you play your cards right."

"Where did you reel her in?"

"Her name is Florence, and she is very nice. She cries a lot, and she's not quite sure what kind of man is right for her at the moment. But that's just how you like them..."

"I asked you where you found her."

"Right across the street. In the bar."

"You didn't have to go far, did you?"

"First she and I are going to the Hippopotamus for a drink. You can have her when we get back, if you're still here."

"Where else would I be? Why can't I have her now?"

"You have to wait a while, my dear... I promised to bring her to the Hippopotamus first. When we come back..."

"All right, I'll be here."

"Don't be mad at me, Fanfan, dearest. This is the only way I can keep you here for more than two days."

"Okay, get out of here."

A Fishing Trip

The Club

IT HAS BEEN months since Madame Saint-Pierre set foot in the Bellevue Circle. She is there now to meet Christina, who is sitting at the back, almost hidden behind a pair of large Japanese screens. It may seem odd that these two women, one French and the other American, should even have met. According to Madame Saint-Pierre, it was at a soirée at the American Embassy, organized by Harry, Christina's husband. They were entertaining an anthropologist, a tall, black woman with a sad but gentle face, a disciple of Margaret Mead; she'd been working for the past dozen years on the mysterious rapport that African people and their American descendents have with death. It hadn't been a very enticing subject, and only a handful of people had shown up in the huge reception hall to welcome this world-renowned specialist in death. One of them was Dr. Louis Mars, who had given a talk—too long, according to some, but nonetheless fascinating—about the role of death in Haitian voodoo. What could have been a somewhat macabre, if not deadly boring, evening turned out to have been a charming event. Christina never laughed so much, and it was largely on account of Madame Saint-Pierre.

After that they became good friends, phoning each other every week and, at least once a month, getting together at a restaurant (usually Chez Gérard, rarely the Bellevue Circle) to keep in touch, or in other words to confide in one another relatively intimately about their personal lives and to share information that each of them, separately, managed to gather about their mutual acquaintances.

"Sorry I'm late," Madame Saint-Pierre says, "but I had to go to my dressmaker's and it took longer than I thought it would..."

"Françoise, I hardly recognized you! I saw you come in and I said to myself, 'Now I wonder who that could be...'"

"Good!"

"You seem so different from the last time we met. Two totally different women. I've never seen anyone change so quickly..."

"All I did was have my hair cut, Christina..."

"No, it's more than that... There's... I don't know what it is... A new kind of vibe coming from you..."

Madame Saint-Pierre gives a juvenile burst of laughter.

"What's going on, Françoise?"

Madame Saint-Pierre smiles. Christina sits back. The waiter comes.

"Just a Perrier for me," says Madame Saint-Pierre.

"You don't even want a sandwich?" Christina asks.

"I'm not hungry."

"You've already eaten?"

"No."

"Are you in love, then?"

Madame Saint-Pierre turns violently red.

"Who with?"

"You don't know him."

Christina's voice takes on the high-pitched tone of pubescence, even though she's closer to the age of menopause.

"Tell me all!"

"I can't, Christina..."

"Oh, I see... He's married."

"No... Worse than that."

"What can be worse than a married man?"

Christina's bright, perceptive eye seems to capture something from the air.

"One of Duvalier's henchmen..."

"Christina! I don't hang out with the secret police..."

"Well, then it's someone from the club. Is it that dentist you hate so much...?"

"No-oo..."

"What was his name, anyway?"

"I said no, it's not him... You're not even warm."

"So tell me... I hate guessing games."

"I can't tell you who he is... I'm too embarrassed, Tina..."

"Oh, come on, Françoise. You're not seventeen anymore."

"No, but he is."

"What? Françoise!"

"What I'm saying is, I've seduced a seventeen-year-old boy..."

The waiter comes back with the Perrier and a slice of lemon. Madame Saint-Pierre puts the lemon in the bottle's mouth and guzzles the entire contents in a single go, a feat that impresses Christina very much.

"That's the kind of thing I've been doing for the past two weeks... I can't do anything the way I used to... Even drinking a glass of water, I have to find a new way to do it... You have no idea, Christina, I think I'm going crazy..."

"It's just that you've finally woken up, my dear... Before you were asleep..."

"How do you know that?"

"I don't know anything... You've just told me... You used to do everything mechanically. Now you have a sense of purpose..."

"That's right, but it's a terrible thing... He's seventeen... He could be my son... He's my dressmaker's son..."

"Is that who you were with just now, before coming here?"

A pause.

"Yes... I hadn't seen him in two days... I couldn't breathe... I drove past the café and he was there. I couldn't help myself... He came out to join me in the car and we drove around a bit. He told me when to turn. I didn't even know where I was. It's a miracle I didn't run over someone... But an unbelievable thing happened to me... I felt like a child who was lost in the forest, and I absolutely had no wish to find the path out... I was reduced to the simplest terms possible, Tina... Nothing mattered but this thing that never gives me a moment of respite. I would feel totally ecstatic one minute, and then the next feel as though I were falling into a bottomless black pit. It's like a clock, you know, that never stops, not even when I'm sleeping... I talk and talk and never say anything... Please, Tina, please don't judge me... Say something, Christina, scold me if you must, but say something..."

"But I'm completely jealous of you, Françoise..."

"Why would you be jealous of something that stops me from living... And I have no idea how it's going to end..."

"Well, until then it's made a new woman of you... You look irresistible... Haven't you seen how all the men at the other tables are looking at you?"

"No, they don't interest me in the slightest. I don't even see them. In fact, I don't see anything. Everything is fuzzy except him. What's happening to me? Why have I never felt like this before, not even when I was younger? I sweat and sweat and it scares me. Can't you smell it, this scent of a woman in her fifties?"

"What are you talking about. The only thing I smell is your Nina Ricci, Françoise."

"You don't understand, how could you! We have the same smell. Oh, his smell... He smells... vegetal, somehow. That's not a perfume, it's his scent... Why has this happened to me in the middle of my menopause? Anyway, so how is June? I saw her playing tennis when I came in; she has a great smash. She's got a good head on her shoulders, that one, Christina... But what about her heart? Has she got a boyfriend?"

"No, there's no one special at the moment, but I'm not getting desperate yet... But you and this boy, have you slept together?"

Madame Saint-Pierre recoils slightly.

"Why do you ask?"

"Oh, no reason..."

"I know you better than that, Christina; you don't say things for no reason... All right, yes, we've... been together twice, so far..."

"And did you come?"

Madame Saint-Pierre's embarrassed laugh. Christina's serious expression.

"The second he touches me..."

"Do you mind if I ask you something?"

"Not at all... But you're beginning to make me nervous. I don't know whether you approve or disapprove."

"Are you passive or active?"

"Active... I'm the one who initiates things, but as soon as I get too close to him everything in me goes haywire... I'm like a mechanical doll that's run amok, I have no control over what I do..."

"Do you have the feeling that even when he's lying passively on his back, he's still the one who's in control?"

Long silence.

"Yes..."

"That's all I wanted to know."

"Why did you want to know that?"

"I can't tell you that because it's not my secret to tell... There's someone else involved in this story..."

"It's your daughter, isn't it? You found her with a boy? Isn't that what you wanted? Ever since she..."

"No, it isn't that! I found her straddling a boy on our verandah... Oh, good Lord, I shouldn't have told you that. I haven't even had the courage to talk to her about it. I don't know what to do about it at all..."

The Club

"We should talk about this again when we have more time... I have an appointment I have to go to... What are you doing Saturday?"

"Riding with June in the morning... What about lunch at Chez Gérard?"

"It's a date. Unless..."

"I'll understand, Françoise."

HARRY IS FINISHING a game when his wife and Madame Saint-Pierre come out. He's winning hands down. Whenever he's ahead of an adversary, it isn't in him to take it easy. He is a lean, mean, killing machine. Madame Saint-Pierre claps her hands. Christina remains silent, a light smile floating on her lips, a sure sign that she is still in love with her husband. Harry comes over to where the women are standing and takes off his T-shirt. He's as red as a boiled lobster. His naked, sweating torso emits an undeniable vitality. An animal vitality. He casts a quick look towards the Bellevue Circle's high green wall. It doesn't last a quarter of a second, but Christina catches it, and when she follows it she sees the young woman who's been waiting for Harry by the gate. They don't usually come here, she thinks. She feels as though she's been slapped in the face. She looks again at the girl before turning her back on her. She's seen her before. Small, compact, tight bum, smooth thighs, very black, just the way Harry likes them. She feels a sexual charge surge through her. The girl isn't hard to look at, she tells herself.

"Damn," says Madame Saint-Pierre... "I left my scarf at the table."

Harry offers to go in and fetch it for her.

"Have a shower while you're in there," Christina tells him.

"I think I will," Harry replies. "Anyway, I'm not going home just yet."

"Oh?" says Christina.

"I have to drop by the office to sign some papers."

"On Saturday?"

"Yes, they need them first thing Monday morning..."

Harry moves off with an easy grace towards the Circle.

Now it's Françoise's turn.

"Excuse me, Christina, Harry will never find my scarf; I left it at Jacqueline's table."

"Jacqueline Widmaier? I didn't see her in there..."

"She was hiding. She's with someone..."

"Who?"

"A young musician she's interested in launching, it seems..."

"She'll never retire, will she..."

"Let me go in after Harry. He'll be making a fool of himself by now. You know how impatient he is..."

It's the kind of remark that should never be made to the wife of a man you've had an affair with. A veil descends over Christina's face. The man Harry was playing tennis with, the dentist they'd talked about earlier, says hello to Christina as he passes. Madame Saint-Pierre takes advantage of the distraction to slip into the Circle. She feels ashamed of herself. Christina is left standing alone on the lawn.

"May I speak with you for a minute, madame... I won't take up too much of your time..."

The Club

Christina turns, slightly taken aback.

"Of course..."

"My name is Tanya... Let me get straight to the point: I'm Harry's mistress... It's my house he stays at when he doesn't come home."

"And why are you telling me this, Tanya?"

"This isn't the first time I've seen you."

"So?"

Christina feels some of her spirit returning.

"You deserve better."

She gives the girl a closer look.

"You want my husband for yourself, is that it?"

Tanya laughs.

"Not at all," she says. "He's not my type..."

Once again, Christina is nonplussed. This girl moves fast. Christina chews her lip, telling herself she could never keep up with her.

"Then what is it you want?"

"Sometimes Harry gives me money."

"No doubt you earn it."

"If you give me the same amount, I'll leave him all to you..."

"How dare you talk to me like this!... Harry can pork every little Negress on the island as far as I care, it has nothing to do with me... People like you, I wouldn't even hire you as a servant..."

"Don't get yourself all worked up. I only came to make you an offer... If you change your mind, let me know... Don't worry, I know where to find you..."

She leaves, moving like a cat. Christina watches her with a certain admiration. What nerve! Suddenly, she feels tears coming on. She squeezes her eyes shut until they hurt to prevent herself from crying. And then Madame Saint-Pierre comes out, smiling.

"Christina, I found out everything... I ran into Jacqueline Widmaier putting on her face in the women's. She always acts like a little tart whenever there's a new man in her life. And each one younger than the last, too. Maybe she can help me with my new relationship... She gets more sharklike all the time. She doesn't bother hiding her teeth anymore. Okay, enough about me. He's a very young musician, as I told you, who has just put out an album that's all the rage these days. You can hear it day and night on the radio, or so I'm told. He's simply brimming with talent, but he's insecure, too, typically male. She told me she practically had to stalk him down, day and night, for a week. It's only been the last few days she's been able to shout his name from the rooftops. Since then he's been sleeping in a little shack Jacqueline owns in Kenscoff. She laughed and told me, 'He's absolutely insatiable, and I'm no spring chicken.' But I noticed her eyes were as bright as buttons. Ah, what a time this is!... But what's up with you? What did that girl want?"

"What girl?"

"Oh, come on, Christina, not you, too! Why does everyone take me for an idiot? Very well, I forgive you. When I saw Harry's little trollop over there I invented the story of the scarf in order to give you time to get rid of her... She has no business hanging around here... I think we have to start putting those people in their proper place."

"Would you give me a lift home?"

"Don't you have your car?"

"I'm not fit to drive... I'll send someone to pick it up..."

"If you're not feeling well, Harry should take you home..."

"You've just told me your story, and I didn't judge you..."

"I'm sorry, Christina... My car's just down there, on the left..."

"I feel so tired all of a sudden..."

"Do you want me to stay with you? We could go to Saint-Marc."

"No, I'll be all right in a few minutes..."

A Mortal Blow

LYING BETWEEN MISSIE'S long, slender legs, employing the same degree of skill that Shoubou, the lead singer of the Tabou Combo, devotes to his microphone, Charlie dips his tongue into the juiciest bit of fruit in Port-au-Prince. Missie never tires of this exotic but exquisitely executed caress. Especially towards the end of the afternoon. She is always the one who insists on it. Missie's sweet, pulpy body. Her sex exhales an odour of ripened fruit. She may be European on the outside, but inside she is pure Caribbean. Her slit smells of guava; her stomach tightens and lifts at the same time, inviting Charlie's tongue to resume its exploratory probe. She moans constantly, frantically, faster and faster, with mounting sweetness and intermittent, delicate puffs of breath. After her violent orgasm (her whole body trembling, nearly drowning in her own saliva), a brutal seizure pervades her entire body and pins her to the tip of Charlie's tongue as she prepares to let herself go anywhere, do anything, lose herself in this timeless, endless madness. The orgasm brought on by Charlie's tongue is for her only the beginning.

Charlie gets up and begins to dress. Missie looks up at him in astonishment.

"Where are you going?"

"I'm going out to eat."

Missie is still writhing and trembling on the bed.

"You can't do this to me."

"Do what to you?"

"Come here..."

"I'm hungry. It's all right for you to go on a diet for a few days. Your ancestors have been stuffing themselves for centuries..."

"What are you talking about? It's not food I want now..."

"Your hunger can wait. Mine can't."

"Why are you bringing all this up now. It's not fair!"

"I don't have time to philosophize with you... I need to eat... Anyway, maybe we can do both at the same time..."

"What do you mean?"

Charlie heads for the door. Missie quickly reaches for her tiny, red dress that is lying on the floor, and catches up to him in the street. If anyone told her a month ago that she'd be running after a man like this she wouldn't have believed it. Especially a man from this part of town. She fully intends to take stock of what has happened to her, someday, when things calm down. That's exactly what she is desperately in need of right now: calm. When she goes home to calm herself, she ends up staring at the ceiling and thinking about Charlie. She even thinks about being with Charlie when she's with him. It's as though there are two Missies: one who is with Charlie, and the other who thinks of being with Charlie.

"Where are we going?"

"Chez Gérard."

"Are you crazy? I'll know everyone there."

"Will your friends be there, too?"

"Not my friends... It's too stuffy for them... It's where all their mothers go. All the good mothers of Bellevue... And it's expensive, so be warned..."

"Doesn't matter to me. You're paying."

"Right," Missie says to herself. She wonders why she puts up with this, and how far she'll let it go. Every day Charlie finds some new way to provoke her. It's like he's constantly playing Russian roulette with her head. So when does the explosion come? Desperately hoping she won't run into anyone she knows, she dutifully scampers after him.

AT CHEZ GÉRARD. A dandified crowd. They are given a good table; the maitre d' knows Missie. They sit. Missie immediately gets up and goes to the washroom. She has just spied the principal of her school, Madame Saint-Pierre, sitting at a corner table chatting with June's mother. The eyes of every businessman in the room follow her speculatively as she crosses the room. She walks slowly towards the back, not wanting to appear to be fleeing, her pert bum bouncing under the red silk above her long legs. Every cognac-soaked man who sees her knows in a second that it is a perfectly formed bum, and that anyone who could attain it, cup it in his hands, would remember that moment for the rest of his life. And all of it going to that little shithead, Charlie, who now, after waiting a few minutes, is tapping at the door to the women's washroom. Missie, smiling and looking nervous, opens the door to him, a tube of lipstick in her hand. Charlie enters and, without a word, pushes her into the narrow enclosure bathed in blue light. He kisses her with his mouth wide open, and his hands feel for her body.

"We can't, not here, my darling. Everyone knows my uncle..."

"That's exactly why I chose this restaurant."

Charlie's hands are already spreading Missie's thighs, sliding up under her red satin slip and holding her by her sweet behind. Twin moons.

"What are you doing? No, not here, I said... We can go to a bar, if you want... What about the Paradise? Okay?"

He gives her no time to continue. He turns her around with a quick movement so that her rear end is towards him, and now he bends her forward so that she has no option but to lean with her hands on the edge of the sink. There is no need for him to lift her short skirt; the magnificence of her superb ass with its two tender orbs is revealed to him in its full glory. His penis is already insistent with a surge of fresh blood. With one hand he feels beneath Missie's ass and unerringly finds the hot, moist entrance to the tightest little vagina on the planet. He parts its fragile lips and, with a single, swift thrust, enters her. Missie is so taken by surprise that, to prevent herself from crying out, she bites her lower lip until it bleeds. Keeping her legs spread as wide as she can, she lowers to her elbows on the sink. Charlie is working her hard, knowing how much she likes being taken roughly from behind. Together they embark on the road whose destination is known only to them. Time no longer exists. Nor the world.

"What's going on in there?" a shrill, vexed voice suddenly calls out. "Are you ever going to come out? Do you think the rest of us can wait indefinitely?"

"It's Madame Saint-Pierre, my school principal!"

Charlie eases off, entering and exiting more slowly as though he intends to stop altogether. It seems a long time to Missie. Madame Saint-Pierre is still knocking on the door.

"Do you want me to stop?"

Missie's frantic face in the mirror.

"No, don't stop, I beg you. Keep fucking me. I'm going to come. Fuck me... Oh, God! It feels so good... I feel like I'm going to die..."

Several minutes later, heedless of the outraged woman's continued knocking at the door, which reaches them as though through a thick cloud, Charlie and Missie reach their climax at the same time, something that happens to them only in unusual places such as this. Charlie's sperm surges in furious spasms deep into Missie's arched body, which he holds tightly against himself with one hand spread across her thin waist, which heaves like that of a wild animal.

A Mortal Blow

A Mouse in the Elevator

CHARLIE IS LYING on his bed, staring up at the ceiling, when Fanfan comes in.

"There was a girl in the elevator... I think she was crying..."

"It was Missie."

"Oh, her! She's not bad at all... Well done, my man..."

"I just told her to go home. She's been hanging around here for three days."

"You want to dump her?"

"It's not even that! I just don't want to change my life for her, Fanfan. Now that she's got a taste for it, she never wants to get out of bed. Meanwhile, I've got other things to do, you know?... I have no doubt that once she's had her fill of me I'll never see her again. That's how it is, my man, I know the rules. Why do women always make such a big hullabaloo?"

"Easy for you to say, you're the one holding all the cards... But wait until there's a new deal, Charlie."

"It's not me she wants, Fanfan. That's the thing... The more time I spend with her, the better off my parents are. Weird, eh? That's the only reason I do it..."

"You still want your dough?" Fanfan asks, taking a few crumpled gourde notes from his pocket.

"No, I'm good," Charlie says, with a small smile.

"You going to the game tonight?"

"Who's playing?"

"Violette versus Don Bosco."

"Pfff... two to nothing for Don Bosco."

"I wouldn't bet on it... Manno Sanon is playing pretty well these days. I saw him when Don Bosco made mincemeat out of Bacardi. And Vorbe has something wrong with his ankle... I'd say two to one for Don Bosco."

"Whoa, slow down a bit... It's the Violette Athletic Club we're talking about here, isn't it? That team could beat Don Bosco with two players missing. Vorbe can stay home if he wants to, my friend..."

"Not since Don Bosco picked up Manno Sanon... What you say may have been right before that..."

"How much you want to bet?"

"I don't want to take your money... I know what the score will be: two to one in favour of Don Bosco. Sanon will score two goals in the first half. Vorbe will score for Violette towards the end of the game."

"If you're so sure of that, should we put a hundred dollars on it?"

Fanfan recoils as though he's been punched in the face. He does a quick calculation: one hundred dollars equals five hundred gourdes. He doesn't have that kind of money. He's sure of winning, though, unless Sanon's sidelined for some unknown reason early in the game, leaving Vorbe alone on the field. Even with his bad ankle that devil is easily capable of scoring a couple of goals. Where would he find the money, anyway? He can't ask his mother for five hundred gourdes. Madame Saint-Pierre would cough it up, he thinks. Fanfan is pretty sure Charlie is betting with Missie's money, otherwise he would have kept it down to his usual twenty gourdes. Fanfan thinks that if he ever did win, Charlie should be the one to pay up.

"I'll go get her, Charlie."

"Get who?"

"Missie... Her eyes glow in the dark. They're like little mouse's eyes."

Charlie seems to weigh the situation for a brief moment.

"Whatever you want... The problem is she doesn't want to leave me. If I didn't tell her it was time to go, she'd never go home at all. I don't know what she sees in this place. Small room, no window..."

"It looks different..."

"Well, she does the dishes and makes the bed... She's made a few improvements on the sly. Sometimes I go out and leave her to it. And when I come back there's always some new thing in the room. She's taking over the place. Doesn't matter how often I tell her this is my sanctuary. She has her big villa, but she wants my room as well. Those people are truly insatiable. That's how they get rich, too. They take whatever there is to be taken."

"I don't know about that, but that was something, anyway, seeing her in the elevator... Those frightened little eyes in the dark..."

"Ah, the poet... I know what you're thinking, Fanfan... You think she's going to give you the money. Well, what I say is you'd be better off getting the money from someone else, and bring me my winnings tomorrow morning. If there's no score, you win, that's how sure I am. Or you can give me three hundred gourdes now, and keep the rest..."

"You want me to pay you before the game... Now you're really off your head... I've got to run, anyway... Get your money ready..."

"Right. Tell her she can come back."

"You suddenly have your doubts?"

"Not at all... But you'd be better off going to see your school principal..."

"See you tomorrow, brother..."

"That you will, my man, see you tomorrow..."

A Mouse in the Elevator

Skin

RETURNING TO THE TABLE, Madame Sainte-Pierre still appears to be in a state of shock.

"I was beginning to think you'd run into your little friend…"

"Oh, don't be silly. He isn't even here… But you'll never guess what did happen, Christina…"

"I'm not even going to try…"

"I couldn't get into the washroom because that niece of Ambassador Abel's was in there being screwed by some man…" she blurted out in a single breath.

"How do you know it was her, Françoise?"

"She passed right in front of us on her way there… I recognized her because I've been to the Abels' a few times. Since his brother died he no longer has guests. And I've often seen her play tennis at the Circle."

"She's a very good tennis player, but she's too aggressive, I think. She's a bit full of herself. June beats her regularly, and she doesn't like it one bit. In my opinion, she's a better player than June, but she doesn't win because she keeps losing her nerve... June uses a bit too much topspin, I think... I think she's changed a lot, lately..."

"But listen to me, Christina. I was standing there at the door, I could hear them as plainly as I can hear you. I was transfixed! I had no idea how well whatever goes on in that washroom can be heard outside... I shudder to think what I might have said myself when I've been in there..."

"What could you hear?"

"Everything! Everything, everything. Everything, I tell you..."

"Well, that must be what's shocked you. You've seemed very edgy these past few days. Are you sure you're not just a tad jealous, perhaps?"

"Why would I be jealous? I didn't even see who she was with. I have no idea what he looks like!"

"He must have come out of the toilet at some point, Françoise..."

"Do you think I stuck around until they were finished? I had Gérard give me the key to the upstairs bathroom and I went up there... Honestly, I didn't see them. But I heard everything. They must be crazy! It sounded like he was slitting her throat. She was making such a terrible noise, I've never heard anything like it before..."

"I'll bet he was sodomizing her..."

"Oh, that girl, she'll do anything. And with everyone here..."

"It was probably the only available place around, don't you think?... When you're desperate, I'd imagine any closed-off

Skin

area will do... People lock themselves in bathrooms to shoot up, I've even seen it done here, so I don't see why they wouldn't fuck in them, too..."

"I don't agree, Christina... If you look hard enough for a proper place you can always find one. Surely she knows someone who lives nearby..."

"But suppose they just came here to have a quiet meal, and then all of a sudden... In a way, it's not much different than needing to pee..."

The stricken yet outraged look on Madame Saint-Pierre's face.

"But we're not animals! At least I hope I'm not," she hastened to add...

"You never know until it happens to you, Françoise... Only those to whom it's happened can say for sure, and I doubt they're about to. I've noticed that around here everybody talks about everything except what's actually important to people. And certainly never to the people to whom it's important."

"I won't spend my life in a place where I feel completely suffocated. You know? There are things I like about this place, but I find it all so secretive. Everyone is related to everyone else. Everyone keeps passing the ball to each other. They have affairs with each other, they play with each other, they even have each other's children. Husbands cheat on their wives with their sisters-in-law. Wives sleep with their fathers-in-law. In the end, everyone sleeps with everyone else."

"That's why it's called the Circle, Françoise. I hardly go there anymore..."

"When I arrived here I was told that Jacqueline Widmaier threw these little so-called intellectual parties, where you could meet the popular young artists of the day. In reality, they were a kind of organized harem. She'd set up these very young people, painters or musicians or poets. Everyone knows that Jacqueline is no more a patron of the arts than you or I, but everyone pretends to swoon over her at those concerts and vernissages she arranges every month... I haven't seen you there very often, I must say..."

"I used to go at the beginning, but as soon as I figured out what they were I haven't set foot in the place... These days if I go at all to the Bellevue Circle it's either to meet someone or because Harry has an important game... He absolutely insists on my being there to watch. Oh, the vanity of our husbands!"

"Do you see that woman over there, at the table near the window?"

"Who?... Oh, her!... I've never seen her before..."

"She's a French journalist... I've heard a really amazing story about her... A friend of Jacques Gabriel's told me about it. She took part in a voodoo wedding without knowing that she was the bride. And Legba was the groom. Yes, you heard me: Legba. Can you imagine? A journalist comes here from Paris to write an article about Port-au-Prince, and ends up marrying a voodoo god. What a country! That's why I stay here. You get so totally disheartened that you want to hang yourself, and then you hear something like that! Where else can you see gods marrying mortals?"

"So what's she doing now?"

Skin

"Nothing... Since then she seems unable to leave the island... Every time she gets ready to go, something prevents her from getting on the plane... Jacqueline tells me she's really questioning everything about her life in Paris. She doesn't know whether she wants to go back there or not. Voodoo gods can change your whole existence. They're not much different from the gods of other religions, except that they act directly and instantaneously. You get the answers to your questions right away."

"God, you seem to know a lot about it."

"I took some courses in it a few years ago, in the ethnology department, with Dr. Louis Mars..."

"You never told me that! Look, she's leaving. What does she do for a living?"

"She works for a big Paris daily. Travels a lot. Writes trendy novels. Goes to museums, galleries, Paris boutiques, you know the kind of thing, but now she finds all that so vapid. Well, she isn't the first. I knew an Englishwoman once who came here and more or less the same thing happened to her. She didn't think she was interested in men, came here from London on vacation with her husband and kids, the whole shebang, and completely lost her head over the first farmer she ran into. She decided to move in with him..."

"You know some strange people, don't you? You should write a book... It would be a laugh..."

"I'm only warning you, my dear, that this isn't a country one leaves easily. Look at me. At first it was still possible, but after just two years it was already too late. This place is like quicksand: the harder you try to get out of it, the deeper you sink."

Christina is watching a green bottle fly as it tries every possible way to drink from her glass without drowning. Finally it lands on the water's surface with its tiny feet. Madame Saint-Pierre stares fixedly in front of her. The two women sit for a long time without speaking.

THE WAITER HAS just placed a dozen chicken thighs in a small wicker basket on the table. Christina signs the bill. June comes in. She greets her mother and Madame Saint-Pierre, wraps several pieces of chicken in a napkin, and begins to move off.

"What are you doing?"

"I've got an early game... Can you pick me up later at the Circle?"

"No, dear, I have to run a few errands before meeting your father."

"My father! Who knows where he is now?" she says, with a knowing look.

Christina lightly bites her lower lip. Madame Saint-Pierre spears a chicken thigh and begins biting into it, which helps her pretend not to have heard June's remark. The girl gives her mother a hug and says goodbye to Madame Saint-Pierre as she heads for the door.

"Christina, you don't seem well... What is it? Is it June?"

Jacqueline Widmaier and her young musician say hello in passing.

Skin

"June has been constantly irritated for some time now."

"Christina, don't tell me she's pregnant!"

"No! What are you trying to do, kill me?... No, it's all because of this boy we have working at the house... I don't know what to do about it..."

"What are you saying? You mean, with a servant!"

"Well, I try to tell myself, he's also a man, and if he's the one she's chosen to be with..."

"No, I can't let you do that! It's not possible!"

"Don't worry about June, Françoise. She may seem timid, but she's got a will of iron. If I tell her not to do something, she plunges right into it."

"I know, Christina, but she's *your* daughter... She can't have a love affair with one of your servants. It's just not done!"

"It's my fault... I've never spent enough time with her. We raised her completely without guidelines. Our time in Port-au-Prince has always been a kind of holiday. When we're in New York we're in a totally regulated world. Everything is organized. It's a complete jungle. I spend all my time telling June not to smile at strangers in the subway, to look out for this and be careful of that... And then, we come to Port-au-Prince. We find this wonderful villa in a beautiful part of town. Nice people invite us to dinner every night. I let my guard down. I've raised my daughter like a savage. To her, a man is a man."

"People here are very attuned to that. What does Harry say?"

"Are you kidding? Harry's so impulsive, he'd probably kill the young man."

"So why not just fire him?"

"You know, I'm really afraid of what June would do... She's totally capable of going with him. At least this way I have a bit of control... I still haven't even talked to her about it... Sometimes I tell myself that all this fuss about social class is a load of crap... Why would it be better if she was sleeping with some little idiot who had a name? In any case, I don't make such distinctions. To me, everyone here is the same. They're all Haitians. What difference does it make if it's this one or that one?"

"You know, deep down you're a racist."

They both laugh. The waiter brings the bill. A little back-and-forthing over who will pay it. This time, it's Madame Saint-Pierre who wins. Suddenly the atmosphere becomes cheerful. Which suggests it's time to leave. There is a lag in the conversation after all the usual subjects are exhausted, all the week's secrets gone over. When the heaviness of life has been replaced by the lightness of adolescence.

"I think I'll take up tennis again."

"I'd really, really like to get a new life. Don't you ever feel as though there's another life waiting for you somewhere out there, that you're not quite in the right house, or the right social class...?"

"Or the right century... I've always dreamed of living in the Renaissance... The balls, the brilliant conversation, the arts, the great patrons, Venice..."

"You know, I used to know a girl at university. Couldn't have been more of a WASP if she tried. Very Manhattan. She came down here before I did. We wrote to each other. When

Skin

Harry was posted here I wrote to her right away, and she was the one who urged me to come. I've been trying to see her ever since I got here. I was told she didn't stay in Port-au-Prince for long, she went up to Artibonite, it's a province... of rice paddies."

"I know. My husband was an agronomist."

"That's where she met a peasant farmer, and ever since then she's lived in this village with her husband and son... growing rice. Can you imagine? This was a girl who spent all her time in museums, went to the theatre, to concerts, all that. I'm truly impressed by people like that, who can make such huge changes in their lives. A hundred-and-eighty-degree turnaround. Can you imagine doing something like that?"

"It's true there's something about this country... Maybe it's the voodoo, I don't know. Anything can happen. You get the feeling you're walking among gods."

"Don't turn around just yet, Françoise."

"What?"

"There's a thin young man who's been watching you for several minutes."

Françoise freezes.

"Where is he?"

"Near the door."

She looks, then turns back.

"It's him," she whispers.

"I thought it might be."

Françoise squeezes her napkin in her fist to stop her hands from trembling.

"You're shaking, Françoise! Good Lord! And with all these people here! This is not a good day for such antics... You go to the washroom, I'll go ask him to leave."

A sharp cry: "No, are you crazy or what?"

Heads turn. She immediately lowers her voice.

"I'm sorry, Christina... I'm the one who's crazy."

"So I see... Let's think about this calmly..."

"I'm going."

"No, wait... I'll come with you... In your state I'd be surprised if you could make it across the room..."

Skin

Traffic

THE HIBISCUS HAS been practically empty for the past two hours. There's no one in it except Albert and two young, uniformed waitresses. The tourists have all left. Ellen is the last to leave the hotel (her face set, wearing sunglasses and a small black dress). Albert drives her to the airport. They maintain a weighty silence during the drive, which Ellen breaks only when she has passed through immigration. She is curious about a remark the inspector made to her.

"He said, 'A tourist never dies.'"

Long silence.

"What did he mean by that, Albert?"

"I'm sure I don't know, madame."

"For once, will you call me Ellen? Please?"

After a pause, Albert at last looks at the tortured mouth that has been speaking to him.

"Be seeing you, Ellen."

"Goodbye, Albert."

He observes the stiffness in her neck. She doesn't like where she's going, he can see that. In a sense, it's her past that awaits her.

SAM AND MAULÉON have been in a secret meeting all morning. Sam is a vulture, only seen when something has already died. Without wanting to make too much of it, Mauléon knows that in this case, what has died is the dream that kept him from caving in when he lived in New York. Today, his dream is a putrid corpse. Which is why he's had Sam in his hair for the past two days. And today the man's made an unacceptable offer. Mauléon tries to stave him off, but Sam has him by the throat. There's no way out. If he turns the offer down, he could lose everything and go to jail (the only option left to him). He feels his brain being constantly bombarded by a stabbing pain. Then, suddenly, the pain lifts. It's as though he's stumbled into the eye of the storm. A heavenly peace settles on him. He hears divine music. And for half a minute his strength comes back in full force; he sees that there is still a way he can hang on to the Hibiscus. Which, of course, in reality, is pure fantasy.

"You'll see, Mauléon. It'll take a while, but I'll get this place up and running again. I told you the hotel business was volatile. You can't blame yourself, you made a superhuman effort... I'll have to change the name of the place, as you know. I've been thinking of an English name, the Yellowbird. It's the title of a great little folk song Harry Belafonte made famous a few years back. What do you think? I can't keep your staff, either. I've already got too many people working at the Marabout. On the other hand, I need a reliable man around here. And the only one who fits that description is you. I'll be spending most of my time at the Marabout's casino for the next few months, and I've got this little nightclub in Delmas

Traffic

that's sucking me dry right now. You'll be my right arm here. I know you, Mauléon, and I'm convinced you're a man of your word. What do you say?"

"Thank you, Sam," Mauléon says, with a knot in his throat, "but I haven't decided what I'm going to do..."

"Surely you're not going back to New York?"

"I don't know... I'm not sure of anything anymore..."

"Don't lose faith, Mauléon... You're like a rock to me... Take my offer... We'll come to terms and I'll leave you in peace."

Hearing him, Mauléon smiles to himself. He knows the old shark will never add so much as a dollar to his offer.

"Well, you know, Sam," he says, "one owner should never work for another owner... That's what the judge told me..."

"What judge?"

"Judge Mauléus. My father."

"Ach, Mauléon, your father's days are long gone... It's not like that anymore. The country's changed. A man's got to survive. And he can't if he doesn't have a job. There's nothing wrong with working for me. You've worked for enough people in New York."

"Sam, you know, this land has been in our family since Independence. General Pétion conferred the development rights to it on one of my ancestors. And here I am, selling it. But there is one thing I'll never do, and that's work on this land as an employee. I will not be a subordinate on Mauléus soil."

"All you Haitians, you've got too much pride. That's what keeps you from getting ahead..."

"I can't argue with you there. At my age, people don't change, Sam..."

Sam laughs heartily. A fat cat's laugh.

"Well, then, let's shake and be done with it... You'll always be welcome here... Will you have a drink with me?"

"I don't drink."

"But it's a significant occasion."

A beat.

"All right, I'll have a small one..."

"Albert!" Sam calls out suddenly. "Bring me two glasses and a bottle of rum..."

HARRY COMES IN with a group of young Haitian women, all friends of Tanya's. They gather at the far end, close to the water, where they can get their legs wet when a large wave comes in. They laugh as they take off their shoes.

What we are seeing is a kind of revolution. Instead of a crowd of white, middle-aged women clustered around a young, black Adonis, we have a clutch of young, black women accompanied by a white man of a certain age.

A waitress comes up to them.

"We'll have the grilled meat, lots of it, and a bottle of 'saddled-and-bridled.'"

The young waitress isn't quick enough to hide her astonishment.

"What's wrong?" Harry asks.

She starts to laugh. Harry smiles. The girls around the table cry out shrilly every time a wave comes up to their ankles.

Traffic

"Did I say something I shouldn't have?"

"No, sir... It's just that I didn't know whites knew about 'saddled-and-bridled.'"

"I'm Haitian."

The young waitress laughs again. Tanya turns around sharply, as though stung by a wasp. Harry is flirting with the little tramp. That's the problem with whites, you have to watch them all the time. They can't seem to get it into their heads that there is also a social hierarchy among blacks. Waitress, heiress, it's all the same to them. An all-inclusive racism. Everyone is equal and everyone is welcome. When in fact they're not interested in anyone.

"I'm thirsty," Tanya calls to the waitress. "Go get me a Coke... Go, go, what are you waiting for?"

"I'm going to take everyone's order at the same time."

"What? What are you telling me? I tell you I want something, and you tell me I can't have it? You go get me a bottle of Coke, and then you come back to take their orders."

"Well," Harry cuts in, "it would be simpler if..."

"You!" Tanya says to Harry. "Your job is to pay."

Harry shuts up. The waitress goes back to the bar.

"Never do that to me again, you hear?... Are you with me or with her? Because I can leave right now if you want, but as long as I'm sitting at this table, I'll make the decisions, not her..."

"You Haitians are so hard on each other."

"And you Americans aren't? When your wife's at the Bellevue Circle, is it her or the waitress who gives the orders?

Would you have the nerve to try to pick up a waitress if your wife were there?"

But now Tanya realizes her mistake. Men like Harry are always trying to pick up waitresses, right under their wives' noses. It's their favourite sport. Harry's laugh puts Tanya back in a good mood.

ALBERT IS STILL totalling the bar receipts when the inspector comes in.

"So, that's it?"

"Yes, sold this morning," Albert replies without looking up from his precious maroon ledger.

"I just saw Sam... What about you?"

"Going home to the Cap. My mother is getting on. She's been living with my sister since my father died. I'll take her back to her own house. It needs some work done on it. Roof needs repairing. And I've still got a few old friends down there."

"You guys from the provinces, I envy you... You can always go back to your childhood..."

"Maybe, but I feel like my life is here in this hotel... If I hadn't come here, I thought of becoming a sailor. I love the sea, foreign countries, languages. That's something I really like... When you come right down to it, this hotel has been the boat I didn't take... Where are you with your inquiry?"

"Everyone's gone home... And I'm not in Criminal Investigation anymore."

"Who took your place?"

"André François. You know him, he's the one who..."

Traffic

"I know him well... So where are you now?"

"I've been sent to help out Yves Nelson at the Department of Commerce. I've worked with him before, he's a good man, but I'd rather spend my time conducting inquiries. The chief said to me the other day that I'd be happy conducting inquiries until the whole force went bankrupt. Really, I don't know what he meant by that, because I only earn a small salary and I pay most of the expenses of an inquiry myself..."

"Will you take a glass of rum? It's the last time I'll be able to offer you one..."

"Of course... Here's to you, old brother..."

The inspector studies the golden liquid in his glass for a long time. Night is beginning to fall. A red sun slides gently into the Gulf of Gonâve.

"Did you finish your inquiry?"

"What do you mean by finish?"

"Did you arrest anyone in the end?"

Silence. The inspector's glass is refilled.

"Now that you mention it, no. I never found out who was guilty... It's hard when you hold an inquiry meant solely to find a guilty party. I met a lot of guilty parties in the course of my inquiry, but none of them were the one I was looking for."

"Did you arrest them anyway?"

"No... it's against my code of ethics. I know there are other inspectors who find things out along the way, but I have a problem with that..."

"You mean to tell me they shouldn't act on what they find out?"

"Not as far as I'm concerned, no."

"What if they're important discoveries, of great benefit, like Fleming when he discovered penicillin when he was looking for something else?"

"If that's not what he was looking for, then he shouldn't have to tell anyone about it. From a strictly ethical point of view."

From the other end of the bar comes the low sound of Harry's laughter and the high shrieks of girls being tickled.

"Your new clientele?"

"He's a friend of Sam's."

"I know who he is," says the inspector. "He's the American consul. Yves told me about him. He's in the business of trafficking passports to any crook who'll supply him with girls. Yves has had to go see him a few times at his cottage in Mariani."

"So, if you found proof positive of something like that, for example, are you saying you wouldn't arrest him?"

"I'm not in the Morality Squad. That's Gérard Henry's division..."

"But you just said he's trafficking in passports..."

"Did I say passports? Sorry, I meant visas... I told Yves there's nothing illegal about it. A consul has the right to issue visas. It's up to him if he wants to open his country's door to every asshole in Port-au-Prince. If it were the other way around, that'd be different..."

"The other way around?"

"If someone was getting his jollies by issuing Haitian visas to every scumbag in New York, then I'd step in... As far as I'm concerned, what goes on in that cottage is private business... Anyway, to be honest, I've got to say I prefer less complicated cases..."

"So what are you going to do now?"

"I don't know... Spend some time with Yves at Commerce, I guess, and if it turns out that that's not my bag I might try taking my chances in Montreal. I've got a cousin up there..."

"You're still young enough to take on something like that... Me, I'm going home..."

The Master's Flesh

I WAS HAVING COFFEE at this woman's place in a ritzy part of Debussy. Tree-lined streets. House discreetly hidden behind a hedge of bougainvillea and hibiscus. Old, middle-class family going back to the colonial period. We were sitting quietly on the verandah. Light breeze. Night slowly coming on.

The old servant comes with the coffee, dragging his feet. A soft, irregular sound. Time stretches on to infinity. I think of Dali's melted watches. When I glance briefly into the large room, there's a full portrait, in oil, of a couple I don't know, at the bottom of the stairs. A tall Negro man standing beside a young white girl. The old woman facing me notices my mild shock, has perhaps even been waiting for it.

"Those are my ancestors," she says in the detached voice of someone who has told this story a number of times already...

"Oh?" I say, this time hiding my surprise.

"He was a former slave, and she was the master's daughter. I think theirs was one of the rare legitimate unions of its kind," she adds, with a certain deliberateness.

"They were married, then?"

208

She looks at me slyly.

"Of course."

"So he managed to seduce the master's daughter, did he?"

"No, it was she who seduced him."

I look again at the portrait. The man has a dignified air. The young woman's knowing smile is the same one I've just seen twice on the face of the old woman sitting across from me.

"Family lore has it," she continues, "she saw him from her window. Her bedroom was on the second floor. He was working at the sugar mill. I imagine his naked torso, covered in perspiration. My forebear was a very muscular man. At that moment she was struck as though by a violent pain in her chest. The release, if I may put it like that, of a very powerful physical emotion. An obscene passion. She was overcome by it. And all the more so as she had to hide her feelings from the world. It was a passion forbidden by the Napoleonic Code. But of course one cannot bid one's heart not to love. Much less one's body. A body is much worse than a heart, Fanfan. Unable to resist any longer, one night she stole down to his hut. It seems they quarrelled the entire night. He pushed her away. She became a madwoman. And she was such a delicate soul. She cried. She clawed at her breast, she slapped his face as hard as she could, she swore at him, she begged him to kiss her, she demanded he make love to her, she threatened to scream and accuse him of trying to rape her, she wept until she had no more tears to weep, she tore her clothes, she begged him, begged him, begged him to take her. He, for his part, was not insensitive to the luminous quality of her fragile, white body, so rarely given to a Negro man, but he knew that if he gave in to her, death would be waiting for him with the rising sun. And so the more violent became her desire for him, the more he resisted. But finally, just before daybreak, he relented and entered her. She cried out while pressing her fist into her mouth. And then he fell asleep, still on top of her."

"And that's how they were found?"

"No. She woke up shortly afterwards, before he did. And they ran away. Of course they didn't get far. Imagine: a slave and a young white woman. The master wanted to kill him with his own hands, but she swore she would stab herself if her father touched a single hair on his head. Two days later, he escaped, alone."

"And they caught him?"

"No. Other events had come up in the meantime. More serious concerns... The War of Independence broke out. Santo Domingo became one vast, raging fire. Dessalines became the leader of the native army. My forebear commanded the Twenty-Second Half-Brigade, in the north. General Dessalines, as you know, carried the war right up to the final battle. They completely routed the army of Napoleon. Glory! Santo Domingo became Haiti on January the first, 1804. Then Dessalines ordered the general massacre of all the French on the island, and my forebear interceded with the commander-in-chief to spare the family of his beloved. Dessalines hesitated, but in the end he agreed, most assuredly in recognition of the heroic actions of my forebear during the final battle at Vertières. The family left Haiti on the first boat leaving for France, but the young woman stayed behind to live with her lover. It's a nice story, don't you think?"

"Very nice."

The old woman suddenly breaks out laughing.

"Do you know what General Dessalines said to my forebear, when he granted him the young woman whose family he had just saved?"

"No."

"He said: 'I see you like the master's flesh.'"

"The master's flesh?"

"That's how he referred to the young girl... Strange, isn't it?"

"Very."

"In the end," she continues, after a moment, "desire is always what drives history."

"You mean love..."

"No," she insists. "I mean sex. The furious desire of the master's flesh..."

There is a long moment of silence.

"I'm a bit tired, Fanfan..."

I took my leave of her. The old servant came, moving as slowly as ever, and opened the gate. As I passed through it, I felt as though I was entering another world.